D0391579

As she shut her locker door, Ivy looked over her shoulder and saw Maya, the new girl, looking in her direction.

Or . . . *Wait a minute.* A chill ran through Ivy as she followed Maya's gaze.

It wasn't Ivy that Maya was looking at. It was *Brendan.* And as Ivy watched, Maya moved towards Brendan's locker. She didn't even seem to see Ivy as she reached out to run one finger along the metal surface, still gazing after Brendan in the distance.

Sink your fangs into these:

MY SISTER THE VAMPIRE

Switched

Fangtastic!

Revamped!

Vampalicious

Take Two

Love Bites

Lucky Break

Star Style

Twin Spins!

Date with Destiny

Flying Solo

Stake Out!

Double Disaster!

Flipping Out

Fashion Frightmare

MY BROTHER THE WEREWOLF

Cry Wolf!

Puppy Love!

Howl-oween!

Tail Spin

Sienna Mercer

MY SISTER THE VAMPIRE

SECRETS & SPiES

EGMONT

With special thanks to Stephanie Burgis

For the real Ivy, with love

EGMONT

We bring stories to life

My Sister the Vampire: Secrets and Spies first published in Great Britain 2014
by Egmont UK Limited, The Yellow Building, 1 Nicholas Road,
London W11 4AN

Copyright © Working Partners Ltd 2014

Created by Working Partners Limited, London WC1X 9HH

ISBN 978 1 4052 6572 0

3 5 7 9 10 8 6 4 2

A CIP catalogue record for this title is available from the British Library

Typeset by Avon DataSet Ltd, Bidford on Avon, Warwickshire B50 4JH
Printed and bound in Great Britain by the CPI Group

54093/3

All rights reserved. No part of this publication may be reproduced, stored in a retrieval system, or transmitted, in any form or by any means, electronic, mechanical, photocopying, recording or otherwise, without the prior permission of the publisher and copyright owner.

Stay safe online. Egmont is not responsible for content hosted by third parties.

EGMONT LUCKY COIN

Our story began over a century ago, when seventeen-year-old Egmont Harald Petersen found a coin in the street.

He was on his way to buy a flyswatter, a small hand-operated printing machine that he then set up in his tiny apartment.

The coin brought him such good luck that today Egmont has offices in over 30 countries around the world. And that lucky coin is still kept at the company's head offices in Denmark.

Chapter One

'You guys *must* see my photos from New York!' Olivia Abbott dived down to grab her digital camera from the sequinned purple bag by her feet. 'Jackson took a bunch of photos in between takes. Seriously, my BF is an *awesome* photographer . . .'

As she sat back up, her hair knocked straight into her sister Ivy Vega's jet-black cellphone and sent it flying through the air.

'Aahhh!'

Something *else* Olivia had brought back from New York City was her outrageously high

1950s-style beehive hairdo, left over from her latest movie shoot for *Eternal Sunset*!

Who knew that historical hair could be dangerous? Olivia thought, as the phone soared through the air towards the wall . . . until Ivy's boyfriend, Brendan, caught it with superhuman agility.

He hunched his shoulders and looked furtively around the room. Luckily, Olivia's adoptive parents were busy admiring the souvenirs she'd just passed on to her new stepmom, Lillian, on the other side of the Vegas' living room. They wouldn't have noticed a jet-plane landing beside them, much less the fact that Brendan had reacted far quicker than any ordinary human being should have.

Olivia knew just what he must be thinking. The First Law of the Night commanded that vampires never, *ever* let humans find out about their existence . . . unless they had an identical twin sister who was a vampire, but that did *not* happen often!

'It's OK,' she whispered to Brendan. 'They didn't notice.'

'Doofus,' Ivy murmured, shaking her head and smiling. Still, she looked relieved as Brendan handed her the phone.

Olivia winced. 'Sorry about that. I didn't mean –'

'I know. It wasn't you, it was your *hair*!' Ivy rolled her kohl-lined eyes. 'Seriously, when are you going to have an update? It hasn't been 1950 for a *long* time.'

'Give me a break!' Olivia laughed as she sat back on the couch beside Ivy, twitching the swirling pink skirt of her dress into place. 'I've been off-set for less than five hours, and back in town for literally twenty minutes.' Carefully, she shook her head, feeling the weight of the piled hair. 'I'll change it as soon as I get a chance, I promise.'

'You'd better.' Ivy crossed her arms over her black-and-crimson, bat-winged shirt. 'Because we look even *less* like twins than usual right now.'

'And that's a problem because . . .?' Olivia began.

Then she caught her sister's meaning. *Ohhh, right!* With such massively different hairstyles, there was no way the two girls would be able to pull one of their occasionally necessary twin-switches. Pretending to be each other had saved their skins more than once.

'I don't know,' Olivia mused, tongue in cheek. 'Maybe if *you* got a beehive hairdo to match mine . . .'

'Glagl-argh-*what*?' Choking, Ivy dropped her phone again.

Olivia burst out laughing, while a grinning

Brendan patted Ivy's shoulder.

'Hey, it might be kind of cute,' he teased.

Ivy let out a moan of pure horror.

Olivia took pity on her grumpy goth vampire twin. 'Just kidding,' she said with a wink. 'My hair will be back to normal by tomorrow.'

'Olivia?' The twins' vampire bio-dad, Charles Vega, crossed the room towards them, elegant as always in a tailored black suit. 'Did you say you had some pictures to show us?'

'That's right!' Olivia bounced up to hand over the camera. 'I took photos all over New York City.'

'Ah, New York . . .' Charles sighed wistfully as he took the camera. 'It's been so long since I was there. Did you go to DeLucci's?'

'Um . . .' Olivia frowned. 'What's that?'

Charles half closed his eyes with an expression of longing. 'It's a famous restaurant,' he said. 'They serve the most mouth-watering steaks

I've ever eaten . . . I used to go straight from there to the Tea Room dance hall. Didn't you even walk past it while you were filming?'

'Sorry.' Olivia shrugged. 'I didn't see either of those places. In fact, I've never even heard of them.'

'Wait . . . that's it!' Olivia's adoptive father, Mr Abbott, clicked his fingers as he walked over to join them. 'I've heard of DeLucci's *and* the Tea Room dance hall. But only in History Channel documentaries about the 1920s.' He shook his head in obvious confusion. 'Charles, both of those places you just mentioned closed down *decades* ago – well before either of us was born!'

Uh-oh. Olivia froze as she realised what had happened.

Her bio-dad was usually so careful . . . but the Abbotts were so much like family to him now, he must have forgotten that they didn't know his Big

Secret. *How is he going to get out of this?*

'Uh . . .' Charles blinked rapidly, looking more rattled than she'd ever seen him. 'Documentaries! That must be it!' He licked his lips, the fingers of his right hand tapping nervously against Olivia's camera. 'I . . . was up late the other night watching documentaries on old New York. The lack of sleep must have confused me.'

'But you just said you'd *been* there,' Mrs Abbott said, drawing closer. 'You gave so many details . . .'

'Yes. Well.' Charles smiled weakly. 'Do you know, for a moment I may have thought they were memories, but of course it must have been just a dream. Too much History Channel for me! Haha?'

'But . . .' Mr Abbott began.

'Olivia!' Lillian Vega stepped forwards quickly, shielding Charles from the others. 'You have to tell me all about the production,' she said, looking as excited as Ivy when a new Pall Bearers album was about to be released. Lillian's job was as an Assistant Director on Hollywood movies – she had first met Charles when one of her movies filmed in Franklin Grove. 'What kind of cameras were they using on-set?'

'Um . . . black ones?' Olivia shrugged, laughing as she sat back down next to Ivy.

Her stepmom frowned. 'But were they film or lightweight DV? And what was the "FPS" rate?'

Ivy snickered. 'From the look on Olivia's face, I think you might as well have just asked that question in Latin!'

'Sorry.' Olivia smiled apologetically. 'If I knew, I would tell you.'

'Oh . . . of course.' Lillian sighed. 'I haven't been on a film set since before the wedding. I was just looking forward to getting some good technical details. Never mind.'

'Well, you know what us thespians are like when it comes to the nitty-gritty of production,' Olivia said lightly. 'It's all magic and fairy lights to us.'

She was hoping to get a laugh . . . but Lillian only looked more depressed.

This is weird. Olivia turned to trade a worried look with Ivy. Their stepmom was usually upbeat around the twins and any guests – always the perfect hostess. What could be going on to make her so morose right now?

Brendan's cellphone broke the awkward silence. He slipped it out of his jeans pocket, took one look, and immediately silenced the call. At the same moment, Lillian suddenly brightened.

'What about the director?' she asked. 'I've heard Tom Taylor can be a bit of a perfectionist. Does he ask for a lot of takes?'

Finally, a question I can answer! 'Ohh, yes.' Olivia

groaned. 'The number of times I had to repeat the same action – just walking into a room, or hanging up a phone! Seriously, how can there be a *wrong way* to hang up a phone?'

'Well . . .' Lillian's face lit up with interest. She leaned forward, as if to respond . . .

. . . But Ivy spoke before she could, looking straight at Charles. 'Now that we're all here and settled down, could you *please* tell us your "big news"?'

Olivia frowned as she saw her stepmom sink back, looking deflated at the interruption, but Ivy didn't seem to notice. She was already turning to Olivia and the Abbotts to explain:

'He's been teasing us with this "upcoming announcement" for the last three days!'

'Ohhh, that's right.' Olivia nodded. 'You sent me that text yesterday saying he had big news, but you never told me what it was.'

'That's because he won't tell anybody!' Ivy growled.

'Until now.' Charles grinned. 'If I may have a drumroll, please . . .'

Brendan made drumming noises on the coffee table with his fingertips, and everyone laughed, gathering close to listen.

Charles cleared his throat. 'Several years ago, I hosted an exhibit of rare, Eastern European fashions at the Franklin Grove museum. It was quite popular at the time, and apparently some people haven't forgotten it . . . so I've now been asked to curate and host another exhibit, on artefacts from the same region!'

'Wow.' Ivy shared a wide-eyed look with Olivia. 'That *is* big news!'

'Congratulations, darling,' Lillian said, and turned to kiss him on the cheek.

'Yes, what an honour,' Mrs Abbott said warmly.

'Good for you, Charles.' Mr Abbott beamed. When he took a deep breath, Olivia rolled her eyes as Ivy grinned at her. Another one of Mr Abbott's *deep* quotes was coming. '"What we are today comes from our thoughts of yesterday, and our present thoughts build our life of tomorrow: Our life is the creation of our mind."'

'Er . . . yes. Thank you.' Charles bowed to the room at large.

Olivia was still fixated on what he'd said first, though. 'You hosted a *fashion* exhibit? I wish I'd been living in Franklin Grove back then to see it!'

'Really?' Charles raised his eyebrows. 'Lots of those dresses are still on display.'

'What?' Olivia sat bolt-upright. 'There are vintage fashions on display in Franklin Grove . . . And no one told *me*?'

Laughing, Ivy nudged her. 'Did you even know there was a museum in this town?'

'That's not the point,' Olivia said, with a mock scowl for her twin.

'Better yet,' Charles added, 'I've also been asked to come up with interior designs for the museum's South Wing.'

'The South Wing?' Mr Abbott frowned. 'What's in there now?'

'Nothing,' Charles said. 'It has been closed for years, but they're thinking of re-opening it if my exhibit is successful. So, I'm pulling out all the stops. I've arranged for the loan of several priceless historical artefacts to be shipped over specially from Transylvania.'

'My goodness.' Mrs Abbott shook her head in wonder. 'How on earth did you manage that?'

'Well, I had some help.' Charles smiled. 'My parents, the Count and Countess Lazar, pulled a few . . . *delicate* strings.'

Olivia grinned at her sister. Sometimes it was

cool having Transylvanian royalty for family.

Brendan's phone rang again. This time, Olivia noticed a definite flash of irritation cross his face, but instead of silencing the phone, he stood up.

'Sorry,' he muttered. He was holding the phone slightly away from his body, as if it were a bomb that might go off. 'I'd better take this.'

The adults barely even seemed to notice.

'You must tell us all about your plans!' Mrs Abbott said to Charles. 'What is your theme going to be?'

But Olivia stopped listening to the adults as Brendan disappeared from the room. Her frown deepened as she heard the front door open and close.

Wait a minute. Why would Brendan bother to go all the way out of the house to take a phone call . . .? Was he trying to make certain he would not be heard, even by the vampires with super-hearing?

Even *Ivy*?

She saw her twin frowning at the closed door, obviously disturbed.

Olivia didn't have time to dwell on her questions, though, as Lillian's smartphone beeped an alert. Stiffening, Lillian stepped back from the other adults and sat down on an armchair near the couch to type a response.

For once, the elegant film-maker looked . . . tired.

Hmm. Olivia looked hard at Lillian for the first time since she'd arrived. It wasn't just her stepmom's eyes that showed the strain. For the first time that Olivia could remember, Lillian's glossy, dark hair looked . . . messy.

I didn't know Lillian's hair was even capable *of being messy!*

As Lillian hunched her shoulders over her phone, a pearl earring shone in one ear . . . but the other ear was blank. *Did she actually forget to put her other earring in?* Olivia frowned.

Then she realised the worst symptom of all: Lillian's flowing sweater was a deep, dark purple . . . but her slimline trousers were green.

Olivia sucked in a gasp. *Her colours are clashing . . . Something is definitely wrong here.* And she knew she had to consult her twin about it.

Olivia leaned in to whisper into Ivy's ear . . .

WHAP!

Her beehive hair slammed into Ivy's face.

'For darkness' sake!' Laughing, Ivy scooted away, her eyes narrowing as she wagged a finger in a mock-warning. 'If I take one more hit, I might just cut your hair myself!'

'Sorry!' Smiling, Olivia put up one hand in reassurance. 'I promise I'll take care of it as soon as I can.' She lowered her voice as she turned to look behind her. 'All I was trying to do was ask you . . .'

Wait a minute.

On the other side of the living room, Charles was still regaling her adoptive parents with his grand plans for the exhibit . . . but there was no sign of Lillian anywhere. She'd slipped away.

Brendan wasn't the only one acting oddly tonight!

Olivia jumped off the couch and headed for the door, her sparkly pink kitten-heel shoes clacking against the polished hardwood floor. The moment that she was out of the living room, she spotted Lillian in the kitchen, sitting at the breakfast counter with her head lowered over her smartphone. *She's still typing that message*, Olivia realised. *How long can this be?*

'Lillian?' she asked. 'Are you OK?'

Lillian's phone landed on the breakfast counter with a thud. 'Wha–? Olivia!' She pressed one hand against her chest. 'I didn't hear you come in.'

'Really?' Olivia stared at her stepmother. 'But . . .' She stopped herself before she could say anything that might embarrass Lillian.

But seriously, Lillian had vampire hearing – *nobody* should have been able to sneak up on her, especially not a human stepdaughter in heels!

How distracted is she? Olivia wondered. *And how serious is this conversation?*

Taking a deep breath, Lillian plastered an obviously fake smile on her face. 'Sorry – you asked me if anything was wrong, didn't you?' Her eyes widened, looking haunted. 'I'm fine. Everything's fine. Nothing to worry about at all.'

'Um . . . are you sure?' Sighing, Olivia pointed to her stepmother's left ear.

Lillian absently lifted a slim hand to her

earring-less ear. 'Well, earrings are hardly important, right?' She let out a dry half-laugh that didn't sound amused. 'I doubt Charles will mind me looking less than perfect.'

Then her gaze dropped back down to the phone, and her face tightened. In a whisper, she added, '. . . If he even notices.'

Olivia stared at her stepmom. *Did she really just say that?*

Charles and Lillian had been married for less than two months. They couldn't be having problems already, could they?

Lillian glanced back up. 'Oh, just look at your face!' She clucked as she stood up and swept towards Olivia. 'I'm sorry, I shouldn't have let you worry. Everything's fine! Really.' She wrapped her arms around Olivia in a warm hug. 'In fact,' she added, 'I will show you just *how* fine everything is.'

Nodding firmly, she gave Olivia one last

squeeze and then marched out of the kitchen and up the stairs. Olivia was left alone in the middle of the kitchen, feeling distinctly *un*-reassured.

First, Brendan had taken that secretive phone call. Now Lillian was acting a little bit out of character.

I've only been gone for a week, Olivia thought. *What's been going on here without me?*

Olivia's bio-dad stepped in behind her, whistling a tune that sounded as if it could have come from the Victorian era . . . which, in his case, was absolutely possible. He broke off as Olivia turned to face him, though, and smiled at her. 'Oh, good! You're here – you can help me carry cakes and drinks in for the others.' He pulled down glasses from the top shelf of the cabinet and handed them to Olivia. 'You've been missing all the fun out there! I've been describing the entire exhibit to everyone – room by room, in *minute* detail.'

'It sounds great,' Olivia said sincerely. She wondered if her bio-dad knew that not *everyone* was in the living room with him, but he looked so excited about his work, she hesitated to bother him with questions. 'I'll be right behind you,' she told him.

'Good, good.' Charles turned to head down the hallway, but as he walked away he called back, 'Would you mind bringing in some cheese?'

'No problem!' Olivia opened the refrigerator, leaned down to open the cheese drawer . . .

. . . And her towering beehive hairdo swept straight across one refrigerator shelf, sending food and Tupperware boxes crashing to the kitchen floor.

Olivia groaned.

Ivy's right. As soon as I get home, I have to do something about this ridiculous *hairstyle!*

Chapter Two

'If you really think you can miss weeks of school with no consequences, simply because of your little "acting" career . . .!'

Hearing Olivia be verbally attacked by the mean guidance counsellor, without being able to step in and help, felt like torture to Ivy.

Come on, Olivia, she urged silently as she passed back and forth outside the closed office door. *Stand up to her!*

Ms Milligan the guidance counsellor was feared all through Franklin Grove High for her vicious lectures. Now it was Olivia's turn to speak, though.

'I have been taking time off school for my acting work, it's true,' Olivia was saying in a calm, confident voice. 'But I've also made sure to get all the reading and homework done for all of my classes. You can check with my teachers, if you like, but they've told me they're happy with my work.'

'Hmm.' Ms Milligan's voice sounded sour, as if that were the *last* thing she wanted to hear.

Take that, Milligan! Ivy cheered silently, feeling very proud of her twin.

But Olivia wasn't finished yet. 'I can absolutely promise that I will not fall behind,' she continued. 'And remember, this is just until I finish this movie. As soon as *Eternal Sunset* wraps, I'm going to put my acting ambitions on hold until I've finished my education.'

'Very commendable,' Ms Milligan muttered,

sounding like she'd bitten into a rotten egg.

It really is, Ivy thought. She wished she could reach through the door to give her sister a hug.

For any young actress, a choice between a normal life and Hollywood stardom would be huge . . . and it had to have been even harder for Olivia since her boyfriend, Jackson Caulfield, just happened to be a megastar, who would continue to travel the world shooting blockbuster movies without her. Ivy didn't know if she would have had the strength to make the same decision in Olivia's place . . .

But she was *very* glad not to be losing her sister again so soon after being reunited with her – and so soon after they'd both finally managed to settle into their new school!

I'm so relieved Olivia is genuinely happy with her decision, Ivy thought. *Otherwise, I'd have to call myself really selfish right now!*

As she turned on her heel to pace back down the hall in front of the office, her gaze landed on an unfamiliar girl hovering nearby, covertly watching everything.

Wait a minute. Coming to a halt, Ivy blinked. *I don't think I've ever seen that girl before.*

People didn't *usually* start new schools in October. But this girl looked the same age as Ivy . . . and one of the few advantages of Ivy's brief, and highly unwanted, stint as Ms Popularity in her new school was that she knew every student, especially those in her own grade.

At one point or another, they almost all sucked up to me, she thought, cringing at the memories. *Thank darkness that's all settled down now!*

But she definitely did not recognise this girl. And, even more oddly, Ivy couldn't figure out what social group the girl belonged to.

With her long auburn hair and pale blue

eyes free of kohl, she definitely wasn't a typical goth . . . but with her plain jeans and dark blue top, she wasn't an obvious bunny, either. And at Franklin Grove High – the most socially divided place Ivy had ever known – the fact that this girl didn't wear group colours meant she was practically an alien!

Inside the office, Ms Milligan had begun to speak again, her tone sharp and angry. 'You may think you've solved everything with your plans, but I'll be keeping my eye on you, Miss Abbott. And believe me, if your academic performance slips, even for a single minute . . .'

Ivy's jaw clenched as she listened. *I'd better go talk to the new girl*, she decided. *Because if I listen to any more of this, I might just go charging in there!*

Forcing a smile, she started forwards. 'Hi,' she said. 'I'm Ivy. Are you new in town?'

'Um . . .' The girl stepped back a pace, but she didn't look nervous. Instead, she looked annoyed. 'Sort of,' she mumbled.

Ivy raised her eyebrows. *What's that supposed to mean?* 'And . . .?' she prompted.

As the silence stretched between them, the other girl sighed. 'I'm Maya,' she muttered, her body language making clear what she was not saying out loud: she did *not* want to be approached unless the school was on fire and she needed directions to the nearest exit.

So much for my distraction! Ivy sighed.

After her first few weeks at school, when the other students had treated her like a rock star, it was a relief not to be fawned over any more. But she'd never before seen a newbie flat-out reject a conversation on their first day of school! Maybe Maya just hated the whole world . . .

No, wait. Ivy stopped herself, taking a deep

breath. *What would Olivia do? Maybe Maya has just moved to Franklin Grove and she's homesick.*

As if thinking of her twin could make her magically appear, the door to Ms Milligan's office swung open, and Olivia stepped outside.

Oh, my darkness, that hair! Ivy had to put one hand over her mouth to hide her grin. Olivia's completely frizzed, staticky hair billowed out from her head and clung to the doorway. The beehive style might be gone, but it had left some seriously scary after-effects that, Olivia insisted, only a trip to the salon could fix.

I can't believe I'm actually looking forward *to going to a salon*, Ivy thought, shaking her head. *There really* is *a first time for everything!*

'All set.' Olivia beamed at her. 'Are you ready for homeroom?'

'Absolutely.' As Ivy walked past Maya, she mumbled, 'See you around.'

It was like talking to a statue. The other girl didn't even blink.

Whatever. Ivy rolled her eyes. *At least I tried!*

Halfway to homeroom, she and Olivia had to split up to collect their things from their lockers. Olivia's own late start at school meant that her locker was not with Ivy and the rest of her class – she'd been placed with the older students. As Ivy waved goodbye to her sister, she turned towards her own locker . . . and smiled when she saw her boyfriend leaning against it, his back turned to her.

'Hey!' Running up behind him, she poked Brendan in the shoulder.

'Ah!' He jumped, dropping the phone in his hand . . . and when a vampire jumped, he really *jumped.* Ivy had to grab his arm to keep him from landing several feet away.

'What's wrong?' she asked.

'Sorry.' Smoothing down his messy dark hair, he gave her a weak smile. 'Just startled. I didn't hear you coming.'

'Really?' Ivy blinked. 'You know, Olivia said Lillian didn't hear her approaching yesterday, too. Maybe there's an epidemic of "vampire deafness" going around!' She snickered . . . but Brendan's expression was blank as he gazed over her shoulder.

'Hey!' Ivy prodded his arm. 'OK, I know that joke was dumb, but a true boyfriend would have given me a pity laugh.'

'Oh.' Brendan gave an obviously forced chuckle. 'Yeah,' he said. 'Good one.' He met her gaze for a moment . . . then looked again back over her shoulder.

Ivy peered up into his face. 'Are you OK?' Stepping closer, she dropped her voice to a bare whisper. 'You've been acting kind of weird ever since yesterday. Was it that phone call you got?'

He swallowed visibly. 'What phone call?'

'"What phone call?"' Ivy stared at him in disbelief. 'Come on. You got a mysterious phone call, and left the house to answer it – and then you came back and said you suddenly "had to go home" just because of some TV show you were missing.'

'Oh. Well.' Brendan ran one hand through his hair, not meeting her eyes. 'That was nothing. I'm just tired . . . And y'know, I had a lot of homework to do yesterday. That English assignment really *bit*.'

Ivy frowned as his gaze drifted back over her shoulder. 'So . . . that's the *only* reason you look so tired today?'

'Yes!' His gaze snapped back to her. 'Definitely. Totally. That's absolutely it.'

'Ohhh-kay . . .' Ivy forced herself to nod, as if

she'd accepted it . . . but her mind was churning.

Brendan is not the type of person to answer a question three times!

She reached out to touch his arm. 'Brendan . . .'

He jumped away before she could touch him, moving hastily to his own locker a few feet away. 'Hey, we should get to class.' He scooped his books out in a rush. 'I don't want to be late, OK?'

'OK.' Biting her lip, Ivy grabbed her own books from her locker.

He started down the hall without her.

It's all right, Ivy told herself. *He's just tired . . . I guess?*

This *really* wasn't like Brendan, the boy who had given her an awesome bat ring, and who had encouraged her to attend an elite school in another country without getting even the slightest bit jealous. As she shut her locker door, she looked over her shoulder and saw Maya, the new girl, looking in her direction.

Or . . . *Wait a minute.* A chill ran through Ivy as she followed Maya's gaze.

It wasn't Ivy that Maya was looking at. It was Brendan. And as Ivy watched, Maya moved towards Brendan's locker. She didn't even seem to see Ivy as she reached out to run one finger along the metal surface, still gazing after Brendan in the distance.

Standing frozen, Ivy replayed her weird conversation with Brendan in her head. He'd kept on looking over her shoulder, hadn't he? It was as if he couldn't look away.

And Maya was still looking right towards him.

Had Brendan actually been stealing looks with Maya?

The answer was a shout straight from Ivy's heart. *Absolutely not!* Brendan would *never* do that!

'Hey,' Olivia called, as she weaved her way

through a stream of students towards Ivy's locker. 'You ready to –' Olivia's eyes narrowed. She put one hand on Ivy's shoulder. 'Are you OK?'

'I'm fine,' Ivy mumbled, without looking around. 'Just fine.'

But even as she followed Olivia in the direction of homeroom, she craned her neck to look backwards, keeping a watchful eye on Maya.

Something weird was definitely going on between Brendan and the new girl . . . and no matter what it took, Ivy was determined to get to the bottom of it.

By the time the bell sounded to signal the end of Chemistry, Ivy was so wired, she could have snapped at any moment. Worse yet, even as all the other students headed straight to the sinks to wash their hands clear of the gunky chemicals they'd been using, Brendan jumped up like he couldn't wait to escape. Shrugging off his lab coat, he grabbed his bag, slung it over his shoulder, and practically ran out of the classroom with unwashed, green chemical-covered hands . . . alone.

Talk about suspicious! Ivy gritted her teeth as she washed her own black-and-red-covered hands in double-quick time.

It's time to practise my investigative reporter skills – on my own boyfriend!

She aimed for the door like a loaded missile heading for its target. Unfortunately, someone hopped in front of her before she could even move three steps.

'Ivy! Hey, Ivy. Hi! I just wanted to introduce myself!' The perky blonde bunny girl who blocked her way grinned hopefully, bouncing on the toes of her pink tennis shoes. 'I'm Marcia!'

'Um . . . hi, Marcia. Nice to meet you, too,' Ivy

fibbed. She had seen this bunny girl plenty of times before, but this was definitely not the time she would have chosen for official introductions! She shifted to the left, shaking her head. 'Sorry, but I'm –'

'Oh, I won't keep you,' Marcia said brightly, even as she sidestepped to stay in front of Ivy. 'But I thought it was definitely time that we met for real, right? Before next week?'

'Uh . . .' Ivy shrugged helplessly. 'I guess? But the thing is, right now I'm –'

'You're Ivy *Vega*, right? And I'm Marcia *Vincent*. So . . .' Marcia flung out her hands, beaming. 'It's fate! Because we're *definitely* going to be paired up for next week's assignments, right? Vega, Vincent – Vincent, Vega!'

'Great.' Ivy forced a smile. Brendan was getting away! All she could see of him now was the back of his head disappearing into the crowd.

She tried a quick sidestep in the other direction, only to have Marcia jump in front of her like a football player making a block.

Is there any way past this girl?

'Marcia . . .'

Marcia grabbed her hand. 'Oh, I'll let you go,' she said. 'But I just want to shake hands first with my . . . new . . . *partner*!' She squealed the last word so high that Ivy's eardrums hurt.

Ow! Sometimes it really did not help to have sensitive vampire hearing.

Ivy's smile was definitely wavering by the time Marcia finished her enthusiastic handshake. The moment Marcia let her go, she lunged for the door . . . only to feel her nose twitch at an odd, pungent scent as she escaped into the hallway. *Where is that coming from?*

Her gaze landed on her own right hand, which was stained with some kind of chemical goo.

Thanks a lot, Marcia!

Apparently, Brendan wasn't the only one who hadn't bothered to wash his hands at the end of their Chemistry lesson. To make it even worse, not only was Marcia's goo foul and sticky, but it was also utterly, inescapably pink.

Bright pink.

Aaagh! Ivy let out a silent scream as she stared at the bubblegum-pink mess on her hand. *No way can I walk around like this*, she realised. *The colour would make me sick even if no one else noticed it!*

Growling, she veered off towards the closest girls' bathroom. Thank darkness, at least no bunnies were there to waylay her this time. As soon as her hands were clean, she hurried back out, stuffing her hands safely in the pockets of her black cargo pants.

Unfortunately, having both hands buried in her pockets made her elbows jut out dangerously from her side . . . which made the crowded hallway into an obstacle course. *Or a really sucky pinball game*, Ivy thought, as a senior football player bumped into her and immediately bounced off, knocked aside by her vampire strength to fall against the closest wall of lockers.

'Hey!' he yelled.

'Watch where you're going!' Another senior glared at her, rubbing his arm where he'd walked straight into her other elbow.

'Sorry,' Ivy mumbled. But she didn't have time to slow down. She shoved the front door open with her foot, training her vampire ears.

Brendan's voice came from the bus stop. 'Look, we need to be careful,' he was muttering to someone. 'If anyone sees us together . . .'

"Us"? Ivy's heartbeat pulsed hard against her skin as she started towards the bus stop. She couldn't see Brendan yet, or hear any response

from whoever he was talking to. *Is he having another secret call on his cellphone?*

Then Brendan said, 'Come on. Don't look at me like that.'

Aha! Ivy sped up until she was almost running. *Mystery Person is right there with him!*

She hurtled through the school gates and raced towards the bus stop . . .

Only to find Brendan standing by himself, his shoulders hunched, staring into space.

Panting, Ivy slowed down. 'Are you OK?'

His head jerked up as he seemed to notice her for the first time. 'Yeah! Of course . . . Why wouldn't I be?'

'Uh . . .' *Because that's the second time today you've blurted three answers to a simple question?* But the words dried up in Ivy's throat, swallowed by sick dread.

She and Brendan had been so happy together

for so long. What could be going wrong now? And *why*?

The school bus ground to a halt in front of them, and Brendan started through the doors with what sounded like a sigh of relief. Ivy followed, her eyes widening as she saw just how crowded it already was from the last school's pick up.

'Hey, kids.' Mrs Henderson, the bunny driver, smiled sympathetically. 'Just take whichever spare seat you can find, OK?'

But there aren't any pairs of seats together! Ivy realised.

Brendan didn't even seem to notice as he sank down next to a stranger. He just turned to stare out the window, oblivious to Ivy's gaze.

Biting her lip, Ivy made her way to an open space on the bench at the very back of the bus.

'Hey, where's your boyfriend?' an older goth girl

called out as she passed. 'You guys have a fight?'

Gritting her teeth, Ivy ignored the question. The bus started up with a lurch just as she reached the back, and she was half thrown into the empty seat. With no space to move, she found herself crunched between a set of happily talking bunny girls and two goths busy arguing about whether the Pall Bearers' new album was better than the one before. For once, she was too distracted to even join in.

As the bus pulled away from Franklin Grove High, she turned to look back at the school through the window. Her gaze caught on an all-too-familiar figure.

Maya stood at the bus stop, staring right at the school bus as it passed her.

No, Ivy realised, her eyes narrowing. Maya wasn't just staring at the bus. She was staring straight at *Brendan*, right in the front of the bus.

Her head swivelled to follow *him* as the bus moved, and she lifted one hand in a half-hearted wave.

Suddenly, Ivy had a horrible certainty that she knew exactly who Brendan had been talking to. But how did he even *know* the new girl?

And why was he keeping it secret from her?

Chapter Three

'Cut!' Camilla yelled. 'Let's try one more . . .'

As everyone around them in the FoodMart turned to stare, Olivia stifled a groan. *Sometimes it isn't easy to be best friends with a budding movie director!*

'What went wrong this time?' she asked.

Camilla frowned intently under her plum-coloured beret. Her blonde curls sprang out around her face, looking wilder than ever after forty-five minutes of tugging at them with every failed take. 'You need to walk *normally*,' she said.

Olivia blinked. 'I thought I was.'

'No.' Camilla shook her head. 'Your "normal" walk is too graceful.'

'Ohhh-kay.' Olivia let out a soft sigh as she hurried back to take her place at the end of the Newspapers & Magazines aisle.

It was a good thing she'd put up with Tom Taylor's 'perfectionism' on set the week before because, otherwise, she'd *never* be able to survive working with her own best friend! Camilla had cornered her just after she'd gotten home from school, dragging her out to the FoodMart to work on . . . work on . . .

Frowning, Olivia came to a sudden stop, ignoring the irritated shoppers wheeling their carts around her. 'What *are* we filming, anyway?' she asked. 'You never actually told me.'

'Oh, it's a music thing.' Camilla bit her lip as she fiddled with her smartphone, adjusting the settings. 'This goth/indie band are inviting young film-makers to submit footage for their new music video. The challenge is, they're insisting it all be recorded on *smartphones.*'

Olivia stared at her in disbelief. 'But you *hate* goth and indie music! You can't even stand being in the same room as it!'

'So?' Camilla shrugged. 'It's going to be amazing publicity for anyone who wins. You'd never believe it from listening to their songs, but they're *huge.*'

'Really?' Olivia felt a prickle of dread. 'Wait a minute. We're not talking about –'

'The Pall Bearers!' Camilla said cheerfully. 'Have you heard of them?'

Olivia stifled a groan. 'You could say that.'

Earlier that year, she'd been guilt-tripped into pretending to be Ivy at a Pall Bearers concert, so that she could get Brendan and Sophia into the show for free. *If only I'd known that the band would invite me on stage.* Olivia could laugh about her "singing debut" now but, at the time, she thought she knew how Ivy's tummy felt when she accidentally took a bit of garlicky pizza.

'Look,' she said. 'Have you really *listened* to their music?' She waved a hand at the rows of newspapers and magazines on the racks beside them. 'I can tell you, footage from a nice local supermarket really isn't going to do it for a goth band that thinks shouting "I hate you" over and over' – *and over!* – 'again is clever.'

'Oh, I've got all of that under control.' Camilla's eyes were flinty with determination. 'I spent *hours* listening to their new song . . .'

And you didn't go crazy? Olivia wondered. She would have needed earplugs and a tranquilliser to get through that torture!

'. . . and here's the thing: it's about a relationship that's ended badly, and it's called

"Yesterday's News". So, if their director has even half a brain, he'll *have* to see the symbolism in all these newspapers and magazines!'

'Uh . . . if you say so.' Olivia sighed. She loved seeing her friend so fired up – but when Camilla was in full flow, there was nothing that could stop her, and no point in arguing. 'Another take?' she offered weakly, taking her place back at the end of the aisle.

'Everyone stand back, please,' Camilla called out. She flung out her left hand to hold back any other shoppers from stepping into the aisle. 'Aaaaand . . . action!'

Olivia started forwards. *Right. Walk normally!* Half-smiling, she let her arms swing gently by her sides. Her chin was up, her eyes fixed somewhere in the middle distance, and her kitten heels clacked against the floor as –

'Cut!' Camilla yelled.

Are you kidding? Olivia swung to face Camilla – but for the first time that night, Camilla wasn't looking at her.

'We have an intruder,' she said, pointing up the aisle.

Olivia turned back to look . . . just as a cute little boy raced past her, giggling. A harassed-looking woman scooped him up and carried him over her shoulder.

'Mommy T-Rex!' the little boy shouted gleefully. He flung his arms around her neck and grinned at the girls over her shoulder. 'Raaar! Raaar!'

Olivia laughed. 'Aww. Why not leave him in the shot? He's adorable.'

'I can't see the Pall Bearers putting out an "adorable" music video,' Camilla said.

Olivia nodded. 'I guess not.'

A minute later, the aisle was finally clear again, with the little boy's roars fading into the distance.

For the twenty-first time that night, Olivia took her place at the end of the aisle. This time, though, Olivia stopped at the magazines halfway down the aisle, idly picking one up and flipping through it.

'Cut!' Camilla looked both annoyed and apologetic as she hurried over, releasing the crowd of shoppers she'd held back until then. 'What's with the improv?'

Olivia shrugged, trying to ignore the glares of all the shoppers who'd been held up for the take. 'It felt right in the moment,' she said.

'We should really keep it simple,' said Camilla. But before she could explain what she meant, her jaw dropped. 'Run!' she gasped.

Olivia didn't even have time to look around before Camilla grabbed her arm and yanked her down the aisle, not slowing down until they'd turned the corner. Then, breathing hard, Camilla hid behind the corner display of birthday cards. She pushed Olivia behind her, and peered back up the aisle they'd come from.

Olivia stood on tiptoes to look over her friend's shoulder. 'What are we looking at?' she whispered.

'Shh!' Camilla waved frantically at her to be quiet.

Olivia opened her mouth to protest, then blinked as a nearly-empty shopping cart turned into their aisle, pushed by a familiar figure.

Lillian.

'Um . . . Camilla?' she whispered into her best friend's ear. 'Why are we hiding from my stepmom?'

'Because I really, really want to talk to her!' Camilla hissed.

Olivia looked at her in disbelief. *Is this some kind of joke?*

But Camilla's face was pale and strained as she stared at Lillian with what could only be described as 'yearning'. She definitely wasn't making a joke.

Gently, Olivia put one hand on her arm. 'We can hardly talk to Lillian from here, can we? Not unless we're going to call her cell.'

Biting her lip, Camilla looked down at the smartphone in her hand. 'Do you think we should?'

Olivia let out a disbelieving half-laugh. 'Camilla, what is *up* with you today?'

'I can't help it,' Camilla groaned, slumping against the rack of birthday cards. 'I just really want to get to know her properly. She's been working in Hollywood for . . . for, like, *forever*.'

Olivia tried not to laugh. *You don't even know how true that is.*

'She could give me so much advice on real film-making,' Camilla said miserably. 'But I just can't make myself talk to her!'

'That's ridiculous.' Olivia rolled her eyes. 'I know you've spoken to her before. What about at the engagement party? Or the wedding? Or –'

'That was different!' Camilla said. 'We were just *chatting* then, about *unimportant* things. If I want to ask her for help and advice, though . . . Well, I want her to take me *seriously*.'

'I'm sure she will.' Olivia nudged Camilla gently, trying to push her back towards the aisle. Over Camilla's shoulder, she could see Lillian coming to a stop to look at the rack of magazines. 'She's really nice. And why wouldn't she take you seriously?'

'Have you even *looked* at me tonight?' Camilla seemed ready to cry. 'I'm shooting footage on a *smartphone*. And, and, and . . . I'm wearing completely the wrong beret!' Camilla tore off her plum-coloured beret and looked at it sadly.

'I need my *black* one when I talk to her. It's my *lucky* beret!'

'Camilla –'

Camilla shook her head, backing away from the aisle where Lillian stood, obliviously browsing a magazine. 'I should go. I've got everything I need for the Pall Bearers' video, so I'm just going to . . . to . . .'

Run away, Olivia finished silently for her friend, as Camilla turned and scuttled off without another word.

Sighing, Olivia started to follow, but then stopped. *Wait a minute*. Something about Lillian's appearance had been niggling at her ever since she'd seen her stepmom turn on to the aisle, but talking with Camilla had distracted her.

What was it?

Frowning, she peered back around the corner display. *Aha.*

Unlike the last time she'd seen Lillian, her stepmom no longer looked 'less-than-perfect'. In fact, Lillian had somehow found a way to look *too* perfect. Flicking through the magazine, in an elegant black twin set and pearls, she looked more like someone who should have been on their way to a fancy vampire banquet, rather than ordinary grocery shopping. Her hair was pulled back by a velvet headband, her make-up was perfectly – and elaborately – applied, and . . . *Are those false eyelashes?!*

Olivia stared in disbelief at Lillian's thick black eyelashes, which were at least half-an-inch longer than usual.

Lillian would have seemed perfectly put together – *for a Hollywood party!* – if it weren't for the glazed look in her eyes. As she put the magazine back and pushed the cart slowly down the aisle, her gaze sailed over the books and newspapers on the shelves, clearly not taking in a single thing. And as for her 'shopping' –

Olivia sucked in a worried breath. There was only one thing in the cart: a big bag of candy. Perfectly normal for some people, maybe, but Lillian *never* ate candy.

What is going on?

As if she were asking herself the same question, Lillian suddenly came to a dead stop, nearly knocking into another woman's cart.

'Are you OK, honey?' the other woman asked. 'You look a little . . . lost.'

'Oh . . . um . . .' Lillian blinked, glancing around as if she'd only just realised she'd turned into the Newspaper & Magazines aisle. 'I'll be fine,' she said. Then she added, in a lower voice, 'I hope so, anyway.'

She's clearly not used to doing a weekly grocery run, Olivia thought. *At least not in the FoodMart.*

Maybe that was it. Maybe Lillian was actually here for the vampires-only secret store hidden beneath the FoodMart. The BloodMart was where the local vampires went to buy their synthetic food. Since she hadn't been in town long, though, maybe she'd forgotten which aisle held the secret door that the vamps used to get there – and of course, she wouldn't be able to ask just any ordinary shopper for directions.

At least I can help her with that part, Olivia thought.

As the other shopper settled in to browse a cookbook, Olivia prepared to slip over and guide her stepmom to Aisle Twelve. She was just about to start forwards when she saw Lillian's gaze suddenly focus on a book in the Life & Style section. She scooped it up from the stand, looked at the front cover – and burst out laughing.

It wasn't happy laughter, though. There was

an edge to it that made Olivia freeze in her hiding place.

Ohh-kay . . . Suddenly, she didn't want to step forwards after all. *This is really weird.*

From her hiding place, she watched Lillian replace the Life & Style book, then wander across to the travel section and pick up something else. This time, Olivia was close enough to see the book's title: *Life Escapes.*

'Oh, that's fabulous!' The other shopper looked up from her cookbook to point at *Life Escapes*, smiling. 'Especially if you're looking for a change of direction.'

'You could say that,' Lillian murmured. She gave a secret smile as she put the book in her cart. The next moment, though, her shoulders slumped and her eyes seemed to glaze over again. With an audible sigh, she hauled the cart around and listlessly continued to another part of the store.

If *Life Escapes* made her smile, what was the book that made her burst out laughing? The moment that her stepmom disappeared from view, Olivia hurried down the aisle, veering around to avoid the other shopper's cart.

Lillian's first book was easy to find – but harder to interpret.

Careers: Fulfilling Your Potential!

Olivia felt a sick feeling of dread in her stomach. Lillian had gone from this to the travel section, hadn't she? Following the same path, Olivia turned to pick up another copy of *Life Escapes.*

Was Lillian planning a vacation? Or . . . was it something much more serious?

'And . . . cut!' Camilla's voice snapped through Olivia's reverie. Her friend had reappeared, phone in hand – and she'd obviously been filming Olivia for the last few minutes.

'Great choice to pick up the travel books!' Camilla declared. 'I take it *all* back about "improv". You were brilliant!'

'Sorry?' Olivia stared at her. 'I thought that you had –'

'Run away?' Camilla grimaced. 'I kind of did. But when I saw Lillian heading in the other direction, I thought I'd come back for just one more take – and I'm so glad I did. You were fabulous! The whole symbolism of "escaping" because of the broken heart . . .' She beamed. '. . . well, it couldn't *be* more perfect for the Pall Bearers video!'

But why does Lillian want to escape? Olivia could barely force a smile as her friend rattled on and on about the music video.

If Lillian was secretly unhappy in Franklin Grove . . . what could Olivia do about it? *I can't say anything to my bio-dad. He'd be devastated!*

As for Ivy . . .

No, Olivia decided. *I can't tell her. Not until I have real proof.* Ivy loved Lillian. The thought that their stepmom might want to leave . . . *I can't scare her like that.*

And as for Camilla . . .

Olivia looked at her friend, who was racing on a mile-a-minute about symbolism, and she sighed. Camilla was too focused on her project to be much help.

It was up to Olivia to keep a careful eye on Lillian . . . and desperately hope that her new stepmom wasn't planning a *real* escape.

Ivy braced herself the next morning as she stood outside the school guidance counsellor's office. It was exactly the same spot where she'd overheard Olivia getting verbally ripped to pieces the day before. *If Ms Milligan hated the nicest person in this school, then what's she going to think of* me*?*

An investigative reporter never let hostile sources get in her way, though, and neither would Ivy. Taking a deep breath, she knocked on the door.

'If it's not a disaster, go away!' the counsellor snapped.

Grimacing, Ivy knocked again.

A loud, pointed sigh sounded inside the room. 'Fine. What is it?'

Forcing a smile, Ivy opened the door and stepped inside.

She almost stepped right back out again as she was met by the ferocious glare of the woman at the desk, an expression that made even Ivy's patented death-squint look like a welcoming smile by comparison.

Wearing a no-nonsense grey trouser suit and *huge* glasses, Ms Milligan had to be at least six feet tall, and from the way she was scowling, she looked ready to expel Ivy right that moment for interrupting her.

Ivy's cheeks were starting to hurt from her fake smile, but she forced herself forwards. If she hadn't been braced for self-defence, she might have laughed when she saw the nameplate on the desk, which read: 'Ms N.O. Milligan.'

Talk about a perfect name, Ivy thought. *She looks like she's never said 'yes' to anything in her life!*

'Well?' Ms Milligan snapped. 'What do you want?'

Ivy cleared her throat. *Vampires don't get scared of humans*, she reminded herself. *Not even the really angry ones.* 'I just wanted to ask – if it's OK,' she added hurriedly, as Ms Milligan's scowl deepened, 'about the new students who've just started here? I was thinking of writing an audition piece for the school newspaper, and I thought I could profile the newbies . . .' Her voice weakened as she saw Ms Milligan wince with obvious distaste.

'Or, um, maybe their . . . their previous hometowns?' With a final burst of determination, Ivy finished: 'It might be a nice way of getting the other students to relate to her – I mean, to *them*!'

There. She finished, almost panting from the effort. *At least one part of that was true*, she consoled herself. She really did want to try to join the school paper.

But Ms Milligan didn't look impressed. 'Unfortunately for your grandiose plans, Miss Vega, the only new student is Olivia Abbott, who I believe is somehow your own sister – *not* that I have *any* interest whatsoever in learning the story of how that could possibly be!' She snorted. 'Believe me, what girls your age think is "like, *so* interesting", you will grow up to find, is actually very, very *dull*.'

Ivy frowned, letting the insult fly straight past her head. 'Are you sure? I could have sworn there was another new girl this week. Maybe –'

'Young lady,' Ms Milligan shook her head wearily, 'I am the *guidance counsellor.* It is my *job* to know this sort of thing. I've worked at this school long enough to know that teenagers have a habit of assuming they know everything, but the truth is, they tend to know *less than nothing.* Now, if you don't mind?' She sat back, picking up a stack of papers. 'I have some *real* work to do.'

Confused, Ivy got up and headed for the office door, her mind ticking over. If Ms Milligan really knew everything, and was so adamant that no one had started at school after Olivia, then who was Maya?

She wasn't watching her step as she stumbled through the door . . . and almost walked straight into another student.

'Hey!' As Ivy blinked, her twin's face swam into view. 'Are you OK?' Olivia asked.

'Olivia?' Ivy shook her head, stepping back. 'What are you doing here?'

'Oh, I just need to have a quick chat with Ms Milligan.' Olivia shrugged. 'It looks like I'll have to take another few days off just before Thanksgiving to wrap up filming on *Eternal Sunset*. I just heard from Jackson, who said that Mr Harker wants us in this town called Pine Wood for the final shoot, so I thought I'd better let her know. But what were *you* doing here?'

'I'll explain later,' Ivy mumbled. 'When I've figured it out myself.' As tempting as it was to confide in her twin, there was no point involving Olivia until she *knew* things really were as weird as they felt. 'I'll catch up with you in the cafeteria . . . but, Olivia?' She winced as she looked back at the closed door of the guidance office. 'You might want to tread lightly with Ms Milligan today.'

'Don't worry.' Olivia gave her usual confident smile. 'Ms Milligan doesn't scare me.'

Wow. Ivy watched with awe as her twin walked happily into the office. *Olivia really is brave.*

Shaking her head, she made her way through the crowded hallway towards the cafeteria for lunch. A beep sounded on her phone. It was a message from Brendan.

See u after lunch, the message read. *I'm in library – need to make start on epic history homework!*

Ivy winced in sympathy as she texted back: *Good luck!*

With Olivia in the guidance office and Brendan in the library, it was going to be a quieter lunch than usual, but at least Sophia was waiting for her at their usual cafeteria table. Ivy's best friend was easy to spot even across the crowded room. Now that her naturally black hair had grown out and pushed her dyed-blonde pixie-cut into a bob, she literally had a hairstyle of two halves. Ivy let out a sigh of relief as she collapsed into the chair next to her.

'Hey, you should hurry if you want to beat the line.' Sophia poked her arm. 'Lunch hour's almost over, didn't you notice?'

'Oh . . . I guess so.' Sighing, Ivy looked over at the queue of students waiting for food. After her ordeal in Ms Milligan's office, the last thing she felt like was fighting her way through the crowd for dry, over-cooked cafeteria burgers.

As she watched the crowd gather near the front of the line, though, her lips twitched into a brief smile. The undeniable centre of attention was a laughing girl who wore a bright cornflower-blue dress paired with an elegant black shrug: Penny, a girl who'd pretended for ages to be a real goth just so she could fit in. With Ivy's encouragement, Penny had finally come out as herself . . . and finally found the acceptance she'd always wanted.

A girl's voice floated through the air. 'But Penny, what do *you* think we should do for the Halloween party?'

'Well . . .' Penny began.

'Penny always has the best ideas!' someone else chimed in.

Penny's smile lit her face.

Turning away, Ivy sighed, her own smile slipping away. It was great to see Penny so happy, but it didn't solve any of Ivy's own problems – like the question of the mysterious New Girl. 'I'm not hungry,' she told Sophia. 'I'll just skip lunch today.'

'Are you serious?' Frowning, Sophia leaned forwards. 'You've got a "preoccupied" look on your face. Is everything OK?'

'Well . . .' Ivy shrugged helplessly, not knowing where to begin.

'Hmm.' Sophia tapped one crimson-polished nail thoughtfully on the table. 'I saw Brendan walking over to the science building just now, and he was wearing the exact same look. Is everything OK between you two?'

Ivy's breath shortened.

The science building was in exactly the opposite direction from the library where Brendan had claimed he was going to be doing his 'epic history homework'.

'I thought it was,' she said slowly. 'But now . . . I'm not so sure.'

There could be a totally reasonable explanation, Ivy told herself. But her heartbeat was suddenly thudding in her ears as she pulled her phone back out to type a new message.

Hey, did you get lost trying to find the library? ☺

Her fingers trembled as she sent the message. *Let's hope the smiley face hides the fact I'm kind of freaking out!*

She couldn't stop drumming her fingers on the table as she waited for a reply. Five minutes later, she was still waiting. It never usually took Brendan more than two minutes to respond to a text.

That's it.

She shoved herself up from the table. 'Gotta go,' she blurted to Sophia.

Ignoring Sophia's worried questions, she almost ran across the cafeteria and through the outer doors. Outside, the sun was shining brightly and students were sprawled across the steps and the field – it was a kind of perfect day, but Ivy barely noticed. She was too busy scanning with her eyes and training her sensitive vampire ears. It only took a moment for her to pick out Brendan's voice from the crowd.

'You have to stop coming here!'

Definitely Brendan . . . and he sounded almost as freaked-out as Ivy felt. From the sound of his voice, he had to be under the fire escape by the rear of the school, behind the Administration building. Flattening herself against the wall, she placed her palms against the brick as she walk-crawled to the edge of the building.

Halfway along, she passed a window, and a flicker of movement caught her eye. Peering through the glass, she found herself looking in on Olivia's meeting with Ms Milligan. Both of them stared back at her open-mouthed.

Ivy just shrugged. There was no way to explain this! She moved on, walk-crawling to the corner.

By now, Brendan was sounding more upset than ever on the other side of the building. 'You're going to cause trouble if you keep doing this – a *lot* of trouble.'

Ivy hesitated at the corner. Did she dare peek around? Or would she be seen? Before she could make up her mind, she heard a girl's voice.

'Do you hate me now?'

Brendan sighed. 'Of course I don't.' His voice softened, and Ivy's hands clenched as she listened. 'I could never hate *you*. You know that. But this . . . is just not the right thing to do.'

What? Ivy wanted to scream. *What isn't right? What aren't you telling me, Brendan?*

Abruptly, his footsteps moved towards her. 'I've got to go,' he muttered.

Ivy dived behind a trash can. From her hiding place, she watched her boyfriend walk, head down, across the school grounds. He still hadn't even touched the cellphone in his pocket, where her message was sitting, totally ignored.

Edging around the corner, Ivy risked one quick look . . . and saw exactly what she'd feared.

Maya stood directly under the fire escape, looking ready to cry.

Ivy lurched back, shrinking behind the trash can until she was completely hidden. Her legs gave out underneath her, and she found herself crumpling to the ground, her stomach churning as if she'd guzzled a week-old garlic smoothie!

She took a deep breath, trying to fight down the nausea that wanted to overcome her. *So this is what real dread and panic feels like*. She'd never felt them before when it came to Brendan . . . because she'd always, always been able to trust him.

Until now.

Chapter Four

'There's no other explanation,' Ivy insisted.

Olivia had seen Ivy make some serious faces before – death-squints aimed at Garrick Stephens, for example – but nothing quite like her expression now. Ivy looked brittle enough to snap at the wrong word or even the gentlest touch.

Ivy ticked off the points on her fingers. 'Brendan's been acting weird, he's been keeping secrets and now he's sneaking around meeting some student-who-isn't-really-a-student. What reasonable explanation could there be?'

Olivia glanced helplessly at Sophia beside her. Their school bus was due to leave at any moment, but the three of them were still huddled in the sheltered spot in the school courtyard where Ivy had dragged them immediately after their last class finished. Sophia looked as disturbed as Olivia felt, but she only shrugged hopelessly.

It was up to Olivia to make an attempt.

'Well,' she began, 'it's true that what's going on doesn't make any sense, but . . . there's just no way that Brendan would be . . .' She broke off. 'I can't even say it – *that's* how ridiculous the whole idea is!'

'She's right.' Sophia moved closer to Ivy, her expression brightening. 'Boys can be stupid sometimes, but not *that* stupid. Imagine the death-squint you'd give him!'

'Exactly,' Olivia laughed, finally daring to wrap one arm around her sister's waist. 'I'm sure there's a perfectly normal explanation for what's going on. We're just having trouble thinking of it right now, that's all.'

'Well . . .' Sighing, Ivy started to lean into Olivia's embrace. Then she suddenly stiffened.

Olivia followed her sister's furious gaze and saw – *Uh-oh* – Maya the new girl walking briskly down the street in front of the school, heading in the direction of Lincoln Vale.

Ivy started forwards.

'Hang on.' Sophia's own eyes narrowed as she pulled Ivy back. 'Before you go chasing after her . . . do you see what's up ahead?' She pointed at a sign a block ahead of Maya, so far away that Olivia could barely make it out. Neither of the two vampires seemed to have any difficulty reading the far-off words, though. 'That's where Franklin Grove becomes Lincoln Vale – the point where we are *no longer in our hometown*.' Sophia emphasised the last words solemnly, crossing her arms. 'Do you remember all the misadventures we've already had in Lincoln Vale this month?'

Ivy grimaced, stepping away from Olivia. 'How could I forget? Skate park disasters . . . the mall where you got that skater-girl haircut –'

'Which turned out surprisingly well,' Sophia pointed out, fluffing her black-and-blonde hair.

'It's true,' Olivia reassured her. 'You look really striking.'

But Ivy's face was grimmer than ever as she glared after Maya. 'If you guys are too scared to go to Lincoln Vale, it's fine,' she said. 'I'll just go it alone.'

'Ivy . . .' Olivia began.

Her twin jerked around to scowl at her. 'Look, this isn't just a potential disaster with my boyfriend. It's also the most mysterious, well, *mystery* I've been able to investigate in ages!

I can't back down now!'

Olivia gently placed a hand on Ivy's shoulder. 'This isn't "investigating",' she said. 'You're thinking about stalking a stranger. That's pretty much "spying".'

'Cool,' Sophia said, then gasped as she realised she wasn't helping.

Ivy didn't seem to notice. 'If I have to spy, I will spy,' she insisted. 'I need to get to the bottom of this.'

Olivia sighed. There was no talking to Ivy when she was in this mood, but maybe if Olivia went along she could keep things from escalating too badly. She gave her twin's shoulder a squeeze. 'Of course I won't let you go it alone. We'll be spies together, investigating the *Curious Case of the Not-a-Student*!'

'More like, the *Bafflement of the Boyfriend Brendan*,' Ivy grumbled. But her lips twitched into half a smile. 'So, you guys are in?'

Olivia linked arms with her twin. 'If you're determined to do something crazy then we'll be crazy with you. Just like always!'

But even as the three girls formed a chain of linked arms, Olivia had to admit to herself that it felt more than a little bit weird to march down the street, *away* from Franklin Grove . . . *And* away from their school bus, which was now leaving the bus stop.

Sophia groaned. 'It's going to take us ages to walk home from Lincoln Vale.'

'I don't care if I have to walk for hours.' Ivy's stony gaze was fixed on Maya's distant figure. 'There's something garlicky going on here, and I need to find out what it is.'

'Um . . . Ivy?' Olivia began tentatively. 'Have you considered asking Brendan directly? It might be easier –'

'– than stalking Maya, or whatever her real name is, down the street,' Sophia finished for her. 'And have you even considered how we're going to explain to our parents why we didn't come home on the school bus today?'

But Ivy didn't answer. Instead, pulling free of the other two girls' arms, she sped up, passing the 'Welcome to Lincoln Vale' sign without a moment's hesitation.

Olivia shared a worried look with Sophia. She could see the same fear in her friend's eyes that she felt herself. If Ivy caught up with Maya in this mood, the results could be disastrous.

I can't let that happen. Taking a deep breath, Olivia hurried to catch up with her twin.

Together, they turned a corner and stepped into a small cul-de-sac of large white houses. Every car parked in a driveway was gleamingly clean and new, and the pets in the fenced front yards all looked like very well-behaved purebreds.

'This place is too perfect,' Sophia muttered.

'Pick up the pace!' Ivy hissed. She pointed ahead to where Maya was slipping through a narrow walkway between two houses. 'We can't lose her now.'

Sophia followed Ivy, while Olivia hurried after them.

Funny how none of the dogs have been barking, Olivia realised, as she looked at all the pets staring as they passed. Most of the dogs hunkered down submissively as Ivy and Sophia walked by.

'I guess they know vampires when they see them,' she mumbled to Ivy and Sophia. *Huh.* There was something about that realisation that niggled at her . . . but she didn't have time to puzzle it out now. It was everything she could do just to keep up with the two vampires ahead of her. The walkway emerged on to a vast town square, dominated at the far end by the massive, glass-walled Lincoln Vale Mall. As Olivia watched, Maya walked straight through the wide front doors.

Squaring her shoulders, Ivy headed for the mall.

Olivia's eyes widened as she followed her sister and Sophia inside. It was her first time at the Lincoln Vale shopping mall, and now that she was here, she could see why Ivy had rated it a solid 'not bad' when Olivia had asked her about it before.

The wide main corridor was lined with goth-themed music stores, and Pall Bearers posters took pride of place in almost every window. *It's like this place was made for Ivy and . . .*

Olivia froze when Maya began to turn away from the CD rack she was inspecting. Then she grabbed Ivy and Sophia's hands, pulling them through the nearest doorway into an indie clothing shop just across from the music store.

'Come on!' she whispered, as the three girls huddled by the display window. Olivia could read the name *Blue Skye's* in backwards lettering on the window. 'This is perfect,' she hissed. 'We can pretend to inspect the clothing . . . while we really keep an eye on Maya.'

Trying to maintain their cover, Olivia picked up a pair of hemp gloves. She held them up against her hands, while Sophia fingered the fabric of a white cotton peasant-style blouse – but Ivy kept her gaze off the clothes, and on the back of Maya's head.

Olivia sneezed at the overpowering aroma of incense as someone swept up behind them. 'My dears! You've come to me just in time!'

'Um . . . excuse me?' Olivia blinked, turned around . . . and blinked even harder, as she took in the sight in front of her.

At least six feet tall and dressed in a floating blue kaftan, the shop owner swept out her arms in exuberant welcome, sending a dozen colourful bracelets and bangles jangling with the movement. Each of her hands was covered with an intricate, looping henna design. Her fizzy red dreadlocks were contained by a pink and black bandana – *barely*.

The shop owner smiled kindly as she looked from one girl to another. 'If you're looking to broaden your fashion palettes, you have absolutely come to the *rightest* place. Perhaps you were guided here!' She held out one strong hennaed hand to shake each of their hands warmly. 'I'm Blue Skye.'

Olivia smiled weakly as she pulled her hand free. *Somehow I'm guessing she wasn't* born *with that name!*

'Now, let me really look at you.' Blue Skye pulled and nudged until she'd arranged all three girls in a row. As they craned their necks to try to keep Maya in sight, she worked her way down the row, sighing. 'It's obvious to me that each of you is stifling yourselves.'

Ivy was fidgeting with impatience, but Blue Skye didn't seem to notice. Making a face, she looked the two vampires up and down, from Ivy's long black skirt and bat-patterned top to Sophia's elegant black wrap dress and black suit-coat.

'I can sense just from looking at you girls that you walk with a great burden on your shoulders . . .' Her voice deepened, sounding dramatic. 'The burden of things that go unsaid!'

Olivia had to stifle a giggle. *Blue Skye doesn't know just how right she is!*

'But luckily, I'm here for you now.' Beaming, Blue Skye clasped her hands before her. 'Now,

I'm not the type of pushy-pusher who would demand a person unleash themselves every day. Not everyone is comfortable putting themselves out there all the time, and I get that. That doesn't mean you can't communicate in other ways, though. That's where *style* comes in. You dig?'

Olivia hoped she would *never* be stuck in a room with both Blue Skye and film studio boss Jacob Harker. That much mellowness in one room might be more than she could handle!

'Now, I would be *thrilled* to show you girls my selection,' Blue Skye continued. 'And don't worry, I won't try to force you to buy anything, or lie to you about how something looks just because I want a sale. That's not my *way*.'

'Um . . . thank you?' Olivia wanted to be polite, but it was hard to know what to say. Beside her, Sophia had turned to the closest rack of clothes . . . but Olivia was pretty sure that was only to hide her broad grin.

'Oh, I have complete faith that once you really start to look around, the *rightest* threads will sing to you. They always do.' Blue Skye's smile somehow got wider.

'Oh, I can't take any more of this!' Ivy erupted. She was standing on her toes now to keep a closer eye on the girl across the hall. 'Is Maya *ever* going to move? Or is she going to stand there forever?'

Blue Skye blinked. 'Are you girls expecting another friend to join us? Because I'd be happy to share my threads with her as well.'

'Um . . .' Olivia took a deep breath for courage. 'Actually,' she said, as gently as she could, 'we really appreciate the offer, but we're just browsing today.'

Blue Skye dropped her hands, her bracelets and bangles clattering loudly. Her smile disappeared as she advanced on Olivia. 'Browsing is like copping out on *life*,' she said, her face flushing red. 'Do you not understand that? Are you not tired of walking a meandering path, not even in zigzags, but loose circles?'

Olivia's mouth dropped open. She stared at Blue Skye in flabbergasted silence. *Where is all her serenity now?*

'OK, we have to go.' Without so much as a glance at Blue Skye, Ivy started for the door. 'Maya's walking away. Come on, guys!'

'Have you not *listened* to a word I told you?' Blue Skye shouted. 'You're following a false path!'

Ducking her head, Olivia scurried after her sister, catching the eye of a uniformed security guard standing nearby with a pained expression. 'Sorry,' he muttered to them as they passed. 'She, uh . . . really doesn't like browsers.'

Sophia snorted. 'We guessed that!'

The shop owner's shouts didn't fade away

until they'd reached the escalator.

Even as Olivia sagged with relief, she couldn't stop herself from laughing. *I'll never think of incense the same way again!*

Still smiling, she stepped off the escalator at the second-floor landing . . . and walked straight into her twin. Ivy had stopped dead.

'I can't believe it,' Ivy said blankly. She turned her head back and forth, her gaze criss-crossing the shifting crowds of shoppers that filled the hall and the food court ahead. 'I've lost track of Maya. How is that even possible? I'm a vam–mmmph!' She broke off just in time, as Olivia and Sophia both leaped to stop her. 'I mean, I'm a *V and she's a human*,' she finished irritably. 'Maya should *not* be giving me the slip like this!'

'Well, the mall *is* crowded,' Sophia pointed out, nudging Ivy away from the top of the escalator. A group of girls with bright shopping bags flooded past them, laughing and talking as they headed for the packed food court. Sophia dropped her voice. 'Maybe the other shoppers are just too big an obstacle?'

'Maybe,' Ivy whispered. 'But . . .' Her voice faded away. With a muffled groan, she spun around in a tight circle again and again, looking frantically in every direction as her eyes grew wider and her expression more tense.

Olivia felt her own chest tightening with anxiety. *This is not Ivy*, she thought. *What's going on?*

Then, Ivy walked to a nearby bench and slumped on to it.

Olivia and Sophia sat down on either side of her. As she watched her sister shake her head and stare into space, Olivia felt a jolt of dread – she had seen Ivy upset and angry before, and she knew what to do in those situations. She had never seen her sister so confused, so . . . *lost.*

'It's going to be OK,' she said. It was the only sentence that came to mind.

Ivy shrugged, seemingly too tired to argue. 'I just hate it when things don't make sense,' she said. 'This whole past year, there have been literally only *two* things in my life that have made any sense: my bonds with you two, and my relationship with Brendan. I just . . .' She took a deep breath, as if she needed a moment to force out her next words. '. . . can't shake the feeling one of those things is going to change.'

'Are you kidding?' Sophia squeezed Ivy's shoulder. 'You're not losing Brendan.'

'There *must* be a logical explanation for all of this,' Olivia insisted. 'We just need to keep our heads, that's all. Brendan is just not the type to –'

'Ivy?' Two voices spoke over them at the same time, interrupting the moment of privacy.

All three girls jerked upright to find Franklin

Grove High's 'It' couple, 'Famelia,' standing just in front of them. Goth-Queen Amelia held hands with Skater King Finn. She had his skateboard tucked under her free arm.

Even in the midst of all her worries, Olivia couldn't help smiling as she looked at them. After all, bringing these two together had been her greatest matchmaking triumph! And she could already see how much they'd changed.

Amelia might still be pale of face and goth of fashion, but the stark black of her old attire was broken up with lashings of fabulous purple now. At Amelia's side, Finn smiled broadly, apparently in a permanent state of bliss. He obviously knew he was in exactly the right place, with exactly the right girl. Even Amelia, who used to wear a stony expression all day long, kept breaking out into sunny grins. Although she regularly corrected herself into a tight smirk, as if she were trying to keep up appearances.

Aw, Olivia thought fondly. *She can't really help herself!*

Amelia's smirk turned into a look of genuine concern, though, as she looked down at Ivy. 'Something's really wrong, isn't it?' she asked.

'Oh . . .' Taking a deep breath, Ivy shook her head, keeping her eyes lowered. 'I'm just being silly, that's all.'

'You need cheering up.' Finn scooped his skateboard out of Amelia's arms and held it out. 'Why don't you give this a try?'

Ivy just stared at him, looking as stunned – and wary – as Olivia felt. *Is he serious?*

Finn wasn't usually the type to be mean or sarcastic, but . . .

Oh, what was I thinking? Meeting Ivy's eyes, Olivia stifled a giggle. *Of course* Finn was genuine in his offer!

The skater-boy grinned, obviously unoffended by her laughter. 'Why not?' he said. 'It'll get the endorphins flowing. My gym teacher says that's a good thing.'

Despite her concern for Ivy, Olivia couldn't help the big, goofy smile that spread across her face. *Lincoln Vale isn't so dangerous after all, is it?* The people of this town might be a kooky bunch, but most of them were sweet.

'Thanks, Finn,' Ivy said, 'but I'll pass this time.'

'If you say so.' Shrugging, he tucked the skateboard under his arm.

'We're on our way to get food,' Amelia said. 'Want to join us?'

'Another time?' Ivy suggested. 'We really need to get back to Franklin Grove.'

'See you at school, then!' Famelia chorused, and the couple headed off, hand in hand, in perfect harmony.

Ivy jumped to her feet. 'We should go home,' she said. 'Right now.'

Without waiting for a reply, she turned around and walked back towards the escalators. The conversation was clearly over.

Sophia shrugged, her expression hopeless. Olivia's own shoulders sagged as she watched Ivy step on to the escalators. Her back was rigidly straight, and her fists were tightly clenched.

She was wound more tightly than ever now their whole crazy mission to find out the truth about Maya had come to nothing. Worse yet, Olivia had no idea how they would even get home from Lincoln Vale.

Most of all, she just couldn't believe that Brendan would ever be *that* boy . . . the one who cheated on his girlfriend. Even if Ivy hadn't been, in Olivia's opinion, pretty much the World's Greatest Human (or *half*-human!), it wouldn't make any sense.

But she couldn't deny that something very strange was going on with Brendan. And she couldn't bear it if he created real heartache for her sister.

Isn't there enough heartache already in our family? Judging by Lillian's recent behaviour . . .

Olivia sighed as she hurried after her twin. Even if Ivy didn't realise it, there were *two* couples in trouble in their own family, now. *I just have to try to help them both!*

Chapter Five

That evening, as twilight spread across Franklin Grove, Ivy started up the steps towards Brendan's house . . . then turned around and walked back down.

Stopping at the bottom step, she closed her eyes, gritting her teeth.

You have to do this, she told herself.

. . . *But what if he tells me it's all true?*

The question brought a strange, heavy feeling to her stomach. It was the same feeling she used to get when her old middle school had served pizzas with garlic, and she'd taken a bite without checking.

Tipping her head forwards, she thought wistfully back to Franklin Grove Middle School. Life had been so much simpler then. The people were nicer, the homework was easier, and she'd spent *a lot* less time wondering whether her boyfriend was a dishonest, lying –

No! Everything in her heart shouted the word. *That's not Brendan!*

Something was definitely going on, though, and, like it or not, Ivy *needed* to know what it was before it drove her completely crazy.

Behind her, the front door opened, making her jump.

'Ivy?' It was Brendan's dad, Marc Daniels. 'What's wrong?'

Oops. Way to look like an idiot, Ivy!

Ivy tried to put on a smile – but it felt fake, even to her. 'Nothing,' she mumbled. 'I was just passing and I thought I'd drop in on Brendan.'

'Come on,' Mr Daniels grinned. 'You can't

have been "just passing". You've walked up to the door and back twice now.'

Ivy winced. It was no wonder vampire kids grew up to be terrible liars, when the grown-ups had super-hearing.

But that was just one more reminder that Brendan actually *had* been lying to her. So he *must* have had *something* to hide . . .

'Are you coming in?' Mr Daniels raised his eyebrows.

'Um . . . no.' Ivy sighed. The conversation she had to have with her boyfriend was definitely not one he'd want his dad to overhear. 'Would you mind calling up to Brendan, and asking him to meet me out here?'

Mr Daniels' smile dropped. He stepped outside, closing the door behind him. 'You're not here to dump him, are you? I know Brendan can sometimes tell stupid jokes but, seriously, he *will* grow out of it. All boys do, eventually.'

Argh. Ivy cringed. *Could this* be *any more awkward?* It was hard enough to work up the nerve to talk with *Brendan* about their relationship, never mind his dad!

'I'm not here to break up with him,' she said, adding silently: *But he might be about to break up with* me.

Anguish shot through her at the thought, but Mr Daniels visibly relaxed. 'That's a relief. We're all very fond of you, Ivy.' Opening the door wide, he stepped back inside. 'Brendan! You have a visitor!'

Brendan clattered down the stairs a moment later . . . and froze as his gaze landed on Ivy, still standing outside.

Aaand . . . that's not the look of a boy who wants to see his girlfriend.

It was another bad sign, but she couldn't turn back now.

'Hey.' She tried to smile. 'Do you feel like taking a walk?'

'I don't know . . .' Brendan's shoulders hunched. 'I've got some homework I really need to do.'

'Oh, come on, son.' Mr Daniels gave him a hearty clap on the back. 'Fresh fall air is *just* the thing to clear out the cobwebs.'

Brendan blinked, looking doubly confused now. 'OK,' he mumbled. 'I'll just get my coat.'

'No need. I'll get it for you.' Mr Daniels ducked into the hallway and returned with Brendan's leather coat. In one motion, he thrust it into Brendan's hands and gently pushed him towards Ivy. 'You kids go have fun!'

Brendan's head was lowered as he joined Ivy, and he didn't meet her eyes. They both waited until the front door had closed behind them before they started walking. Instinctively, Ivy reached out to hold Brendan's hand . . . but her fingers only found his forearm. Both of his hands were buried in his pockets – completely un-holdable.

This is officially the most tense I have ever seen him, she realised, swallowing hard. *There really must be something worth worrying about.*

Trying to look casual, she said, 'Is there anything you want to . . . talk over?'

Brendan shot her a dark look. 'What do you mean?'

Ivy tried to keep her voice level. 'It's just seemed like you have something on your mind lately. If you ever wanted to talk about anything . . . well, you know I'm here for you, right?'

Brendan's lips curved into a smile that looked somewhere between touched and confused. 'Of course I do,' he said. 'You don't need to prove yourself to me.'

Aw! Ivy was already automatically reaching out to take his hand when she remembered and yanked hers back. 'I'm glad to hear that,' she said, forging forwards. 'I hope you feel like you can always talk to me, no matter what it's about . . .' She took a deep breath. 'And no matter how difficult it might be.'

'OK . . .' Brendan came to a dead stop and stared at her. 'What's *really* going on here?'

'Nothing!' Ivy clenched her hands into fists, fighting down her panic. 'It's just that, with us starting high school, I know everything can get thrown up into the air. I don't want things between us to . . . change.' Her voice cracked on the last word, and she clenched her jaw as she went on: 'And talking – *clear communication* – is the way to keep our relationship from changing, right?'

Brendan held her gaze for a long, tense moment. Then he let out a sigh, nodding slowly.

'You're right,' he said. 'I guess it's time.'

Ivy's pulse began beating hard against her skin. 'Time for what?'

But Brendan was already walking down the street, and she had to hurry to catch up with him. He had taken out his phone to type out a rapid text message to someone. Then he looked at Ivy. 'It's time to go to my family's crypt.'

Ivy stopped dead in her tracks. 'Um . . . *What?!*'

Brendan didn't even turn around as he mumbled, 'There are some things that you need to know.'

Like what? Ivy wanted to demand. But she bit back the question as she followed him down the street. *He's finally ready to give some answers . . . so I'll wait to let him do it.*

It was only a ten-minute walk from Brendan's house to the massive gates of Franklin Grove Memorial Cemetery, but with every passing moment, Ivy felt even more confused. When they walked through the gates in the growing darkness, she had to fight back a shudder. Vampire or not, the idea of something she *needed* to know being in a crypt . . . *Well, that's more than a little creepy!*

Less than five minutes later, they were deep in the centre of the cemetery, facing the low, stone crypt of the Daniels family. As usual, the ancient building seemed to be sinking into the ground. Three looming arches, supported by ivy-entwined pillars, formed a darkened awning. A large stone door stood beneath the centre arch, surrounded by tarnished and scowling bronze gargoyles on either side.

In the middle of the door, an ornate square plate was carved into the stone, inscribed with a single, glowing word:

DANIELS

Ivy took a deep breath, fighting down the goosebumps that wanted to prickle across her arms.

This is ridiculous, she told herself. *I've been here plenty of times. There's nothing to be scared of.*

But she'd never been brought here to be told deep, dark family secrets before . . . and Brendan had never acted quite so *mysterious* before.

As she waited, Brendan ducked under the awning and reached out to the gargoyle on the right, turning one of its giant claws.

Dull clicks and thuds echoed through the ancient stone. Finally, the enormous door slid open . . . and a shudder rippled through Ivy's body.

When Brendan had brought her here before, it had felt *fun*-creepy, but now . . . it just felt *creepy*-creepy.

Clenching her fists more tightly, she forced

down the wave of panic. *Come on. A vampire scared inside a cemetery? How crazy is that?*

Breathing deeply, she followed Brendan down the bumpy, uneven steps into the darkness. Brendan pulled out a matchbox from the corner of the stairway and lit one match after another with practised ease to light their way. The tiny flames sent leaping shadows across his face.

When they stepped into the crypt's vast antechamber, with its cathedral-like ceiling and grooved floor, he moved to light the tall candles all around the room . . . and Ivy finally ran out of patience.

'Are you *ever* going to tell me why you've brought me here?'

'You'll see.' Looking completely unruffled by her outburst, Brendan pointed to the passage on the left, where the urns of his relatives were displayed. 'It's all in here,' he said.

Ivy followed him into the passage, where a collection of ornate stone containers sat, each on its own little shelf, rising from the floor to the ceiling. The musty smell was overpowering – but that wasn't what made Ivy gasp.

The urn in the centre read:

MARC DANIELS

. . . Brendan's father!

Swallowing hard, Ivy backed away. 'What's going on?' Her voice came out as a squeak.

'It's . . . kind of a family tradition.' Brendan shrugged, looking embarrassed. 'See, in our family, once you reach one hundred years old, one of these is made for you. It's supposed to be an honour.'

'Really?' Ivy blinked, taking deep, slow breaths and trying to see it that way. 'I'd never heard of families doing that.'

'Oh, well . . .' Brendan gave her a wry, teasing

grin. 'I'm sure the "posh" vampires, like your family, do things differently.'

'Shut up!' Ivy almost laughed, but she forced herself to scowl instead. 'You're not going to charm your way out of this.'

'I know.' Looking grave, Brendan stepped closer to her. 'Please,' he said. 'Look again at the urns. What do you see?'

Sighing, Ivy turned back to the 'Marc Daniels' urn. It stood just beside another urn engraved with the name 'Carla Daniels'.

She frowned. 'Who's Carla Daniels? I've never heard of her.'

'She's my mother,' said a new voice, just behind them.

Ivy jumped almost high enough to graze her head on the ceiling. *How could I have missed someone creeping up on us?* But she knew the answer. The cemetery, then the shadowy underground crypt

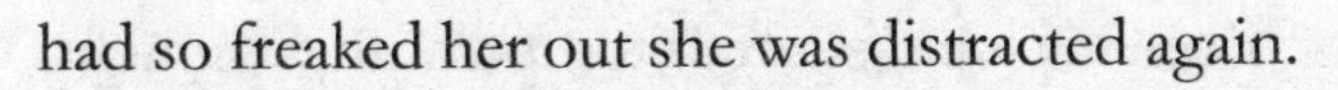

had so freaked her out she was distracted again.

I am the worst vampire in the world.

Gritting her teeth, she turned to face the block of shadows behind her. A slim figure shifted in the darkness. Out of the shadow stepped . . .

Maya!

Ivy gasped as she recognised the girl in front of her, and realised that the not-a-student had been wearing a disguise all along.

Maya no longer had auburn hair or pale blue eyes. Wigs and contact lenses must have covered both of those. Now, as she stepped forwards into the candlelight, Ivy saw jet-black hair falling around the girl's shoulders, while her fluorescent green eyes gleamed.

Only a vampire could have eyes that bright and that unnatural.

'Wait a minute.' Ivy frowned. 'Your mother is a Daniels?' *But that means . . .*

Even as she started to form the thought, Brendan was already nodding. 'This is my cousin Maya. Her mom is my dad's sister.'

'Ohhhh!' Ivy's sigh of relief was so huge, it left her sagging. Suddenly, everything made *sense*!

That was why the pets in Lincoln Vale hadn't barked as Maya had gone past – they'd been frightened by her, just like they were by every vampire! And best of all . . .

'Thank darkness,' she said on a gasp, 'you're not seeing someone else!'

'*What?*' Brendan's mouth dropped open as he stared at her. 'You thought I was *cheating* on you? I would never, *ever*–!'

'I know!' Ivy said hastily. 'I mean, I realise now that it was ridiculous. But come on, you've been acting so strange this week, and you kept on sneaking off to meet Maya in secret.'

Brendan flushed. 'You knew about that?'

Ivy rolled her eyes. 'I'm a vampire, remember? Did you really think I wouldn't overhear you guys at some point?'

'Um . . .' Brendan looked to the ground.

Maya winced. 'Ah, sorry about that. I probably should have mentioned on the phone. I caught Ivy and a couple of her friends trying to follow me this afternoon. They were obviously suspicious of something.'

'Of course we were. All those secret phone calls, the hidden meetings . . .' Ivy looked between the two of them, shaking her head. 'What else was I supposed to think?'

'Not *that*!' Brendan muttered.

Ivy put her hands on her hips. 'The point is, you've been keeping secrets with someone else – and you *still are*.'

'OK.' Brendan let out a tired sigh, his shoulders relaxing. 'Maya's my cousin on my dad's side, but her mom – Carla – was banished from Franklin Grove a long time ago.'

'Why?' Ivy asked.

'Oh . . .' He shrugged, looking uncomfortable. 'It was just this silly disagreement she had with my dad.'

Ivy frowned. 'But what was it about?'

'It happened a *long* time ago,' Maya said quickly, 'and it was no big deal, anyway. She only broke the Twenty-First Law of the Night – it wasn't like it was even one of the major ones.'

'The *Twenty-First* Law of the Night?' Ivy stared at her. 'I never even heard of that. How many Laws *are* there?'

'Who knows?' Brendan shook his head. 'All I know is, after about the Eighth Law, they get a little *too* strict.'

'Anyway,' Maya took over the conversation. 'That's why I came to your school. I had to reach out to Brendan, to see what we could do together to get my family allowed back into Franklin Grove. Mom misses this town so much, it's making her miserable.'

'Aha.' Ivy breathed a small sigh of relief as the last mystery was cleared up. 'So that's why the guidance counsellor didn't know about you – because you were never actually registered.'

'Right . . .' Maya hesitated, looking uncomfortable. 'Look, I knew it was a disaster when I bumped into you near that office.'

'You two actually bumped into each other?' Brendan groaned and pushed one hand through his hair. 'Our school is, like, *allergic* to secrets.'

Maya ignored him. 'But seriously, Ivy, I never meant to come between you and Brendan.' She shot Brendan a teasing look. 'Do you know that my cousin talks about you all . . . the . . . time?'

Oh, no. Don't blush. Do NOT blush! Ivy ordered

herself. *Too late*. She could feel her cheeks burning.

Luckily, neither Brendan nor Maya seemed to have noticed in the candlelight.

'Unfortunately, our plan isn't going all that well,' Brendan said. 'My dad's going to need a lot more convincing before he backs down.' He gave his cousin a guilty look. 'Sorry, Maya.'

'I almost don't want to ask,' Ivy said, 'but what *is* the Twenty-First Law of the Night?'

Maya's shoulders slumped. 'I wish I knew,' she whispered. 'It's caused so much trouble for my family but no one's ever even told me what it is.'

'What about you?' Ivy turned to Brendan, but he was already shaking his head.

'It all happened before I was born,' he said. 'Even when my dad told me the story, all he'd say about it was, "Rules are rules." '

Ouch. Ivy glanced between Maya's forlorn expression and Brendan's look of deep frustration.

'Well, you know me,' she said, trying to sound bright and breezy for their benefit. 'I can never leave a good mystery alone – what kind of investigative reporter would I be if I could?'

'What can you do?' Maya asked, looking doubtful.

'I don't know yet,' Ivy replied, honestly.

Brendan grinned at them both. 'If anyone can figure this out,' he said, 'it's Ivy.'

Ivy felt a swell of determination at her boyfriend's words. She *had* to put the Daniels family back together – for the sake of Marc and Carla just as much as Brendan and Maya. If there was one thing Ivy knew from experience, it was that it was *never* good for siblings to be estranged!

As Maya started out of the tomb ahead of them, Ivy turned to Brendan, feeling a tingle of sudden nerves race through her. She'd started out this night so confused and angry, ready to end their whole relationship if her suspicions were realised. Now they were alone again for the first time since the whole truth had come out – even the fact that she'd followed Maya to the mall that afternoon.

He just has to understand. She took a deep breath . . .

And Brendan's arms closed tightly around her, warm and strong and familiar, pulling her into his hug. 'How could you ever think I would cheat on you?'

Ivy's eyes stung as she hugged him back. 'I thought I'd lost you,' she whispered into his hair.

Brendan's reply was muffled, but she heard it clearly: 'You could never lose me, Ivy Vega. I'm yours.'

Chapter Six

The sky was already fully dark when Olivia arrived at Franklin Grove Museum that evening. Located on the outer edge of the town centre, the massive museum hulked like a Gothic mansion, complete with stone turrets that loomed against the night sky.

Talk about a vamp-y atmosphere!

Olivia took a deep breath as she stopped in front of the giant oak front door. *I'm only two blocks from the Meat and Greet and Mr Smoothie's*, she reminded herself. *There are lots of people nearby.*

She reached out and grabbed the big brass knocker on the door.

THUMP! THUMP!

The heavy knocks echoed ominously in her ears.

A moment later, the door opened with a long, slow *creeeeak*.

'What do you want?' a voice snarled. The inner hallway was so dark, Olivia couldn't even see who was speaking. Then he stepped up to peer out of the doorway, and she sucked in a breath of pure shock.

The man facing her was tall and deathly pale, wearing a jogging outfit stained with muck, dust and paint-splatters.

I can't believe it, Olivia thought. *Am I actually standing face-to-face with a vampire handyman?*

'Well?' he demanded, scowling. 'The museum is closed.'

Olivia gathered herself together and smiled winningly. 'Is my father here?'

The man narrowed his eyes at her, obviously taking in her pale pink twin-set and sparkle-encrusted blue jeans. 'I really doubt that *your* father is here. You must have the wrong building.'

'No, I don't!' Olivia grabbed the edge of the door as he started to swing it closed. 'I'm looking for Charles Vega.'

The man blinked. '*Really?*'

Olivia nodded, trying to look as honest as possible . . . because there was no way she could pretend to be a vampire in this outfit.

Her 'honest face' must have worked, because the man sighed and turned around. 'Hey, Chas!' he yelled. 'Your daughter's here. And she's *pink*!'

Olivia had to bite her lip to hold back her giggles. It was hilarious that *anyone* could get away with calling her formal bio-dad 'Chas'!

'Olivia!' Charles appeared at the door a moment later, beaming and elegant in a tailored black suit. 'Forgive the mess of me,' he said, reaching out to draw her in. 'I've been hard at work on this weekend's exhibition *and* my designs for what I'll do with the South Wing as soon as it's turned over to me.'

What mess? Olivia wondered. She looked again at her dad's perfect outfit, free of any paint stains or plaster.

Aha. He'd pulled his tie loose from his throat. *Yeah, talk about getting really messy!*

Grinning, she tucked her hand into his arm and walked beside him through the long, echoing rooms of the museum. Most of the lights were turned off, and without Charles by her side, she would have stumbled more than once. Dust-sheets covered the artefacts they passed, turning them into creepy, shapeless shadows in the darkness. The ceiling rose high above them, like the vault of a dark cathedral, while their footsteps sent hollow echoes thudding through the night.

I'm walking through a dark, creepy building in the company of a vampire, Olivia thought, *and I'm not scared at all. How cool is that?*

She had to do a quick two-step to keep herself from walking into a dark figure covered in a dust cloth – maybe a suit of armour? Either that or a mannequin . . .

'Hey, where are those vintage fashions you mentioned before?' she asked.

Charles's smile could be heard in his voice. 'I'll show you later, I promise – once things have calmed down here.'

'Yeah, there does seem to be a lot of work going on right now.' Thinking of the handyman she'd met, Olivia's lips twitched. 'I can't believe anyone ever calls you "Chas"!'

'Well . . .' Charles coughed. 'You have to understand, I've known Albert for a very long time. We were rather wild together back in New York at the turn of the twentieth century, before we both matured and settled down.'

'Really?' Olivia shook her head in wonder. *I can't imagine my bio-dad ever being wild!*

He nodded stiffly. 'The point is, there are certain things that certain friends can get away with, even if . . . well, ah . . . in this instance it's an affectionate nickname. Even though it does drive me crazy!'

'I'm not surprised.' Olivia gave her dad's arm an affectionate squeeze. Charles was so proper and upright, yet he still cared so much for his friends. It was part of why she loved him . . . and why she had to be brave now, no matter how uncomfortable it felt.

'There is something I wanted to talk to you about,' she said, as he led her under a low archway. 'I feel kind of weird bringing it up, I know you think I'm probably too young for this stuff, but –'

'And here we are!' Sweeping out his arm, Charles flicked a switch on the wall. Suddenly, light illuminated the vast room spread out before them, with electric candles set all along the wall and a massive chandelier in the centre of the high, vaulted ceiling. 'The main display room of the museum – and as you can see, none of *these* artefacts are hidden behind dust-sheets!'

'Oh, wow.' Olivia blinked as she looked around, her eyes adjusting to the sudden light . . . and the massive, sparkling collection of glass cases, paintings and sculptures that filled the room.

Charles smiled in obvious satisfaction. 'I've shared a room with these artefacts since yesterday morning, but they still take my breath away every time.'

Shaking her head in wonder, Olivia leaned

closer to the nearest case. 'Is that really thirteenth-century?'

'A fragment from a lost citadel.' Charles beamed. 'And did you see that Byzantine Triptych?'

'It's great,' Olivia said honestly. 'But that isn't what I'm here for tonight. The truth is . . .' Her fingers twisted together as she forced herself to finish: 'I really want to know if Lillian is OK.'

It was too late. Her bio-dad's gaze had already fixed on a marble statue, and his eyes had glazed. 'Of course,' he muttered to himself. 'Of course. The statue of Vladymore should *never* have gone here. What was I thinking? I should have put it next to the terracotta urn!' He pushed past her, tutting to himself. 'What a fool I've been!'

'Dad . . .' Olivia began.

But it was no use. He was already pacing through the aisles of his exhibit, his eyebrows scrunched in concentration. 'If I shifted the reliquary next to the casket . . .'

Olivia sighed. The last time she'd seen her bio-dad like this, he'd been in Groomzilla-mode, getting ready for his wedding. Back then, she'd found his single-focus mode kind of charming. Now, though . . .

She bit her lip. Could *this* have something to do with how Lillian had been acting this week? If he'd been ignoring his wife to spend all his time with a bunch of old artefacts in a creepy house in the middle of town, it was no wonder Lillian had gotten so depressed.

I can't let this go. Steeling herself, Olivia marched up to him. 'Can I talk to you, please? It's important.'

'Of course, of course.' Charles didn't take his eyes off the medieval artefacts in front of him. Even as he answered, he was pulling out a tiny notebook and a gold pen from his pocket. 'I'll be right with you in . . . no, no, *no*! These descriptive cards have been mistranslated! Those idiots! Sorry . . .'

He stopped, breathing hard, as he seemed to finally remember Olivia. 'Sorry,' he repeated. 'I don't mean to be rude, I'm just a little stressed about this exhibit. Please, can you just sit tight for a moment? I'll be right back – and once I'm back, I promise I will give you my full attention.'

Without waiting for an answer, he scooped up two handfuls of the descriptive cards from beneath their artefacts and hurried out of the room, muttering to himself, 'As if medieval Transylvanian is even *difficult*!'

Drat. Olivia's hope deflated like a popped balloon as her bio-dad disappeared, leaving her alone in the massive, echoing room. So much for her great attempt!

But then again, what am I even going to say? She

groaned. *How do you tell your own father that you think his new wife is unhappy?*

Squaring her shoulders, she braced herself. *I've got at least ten minutes to figure this out.* Maybe all her acting experience would finally come in handy! She could improv by herself for a few minutes, and have a perfect 'scene' to play out with her bio-dad by the time he got back.

And . . . action!

'Dad,' she said out loud, to the room full of artefacts, 'this is a difficult thing to bring up, and you might even think it's inappropriate coming from a daughter – especially one as young as me – but . . . I know this may seem out of the blue, but I really think you might be missing something about Lillian. I mean, shouldn't she be happy and content so soon after that gorgeous wedding? But she's not, and that scares me a lot more than any spooky old buildings or vampires in jogging outfits. Because if she really is so unhappy that she's fantasising about escaping, I just don't know what I can do to make it right. That's why I need *your* help . . .'

'Help with what?' Charles's voice spoke just behind her, making her jump.

'Oh!' Putting one hand to her throat, Olivia waited for her heartbeat to slow down. 'I didn't hear you coming.'

Why am I the only one without vampire hearing?

He frowned at her quizzically. 'Were you . . . *talking* to the artefacts?'

'I was practising for you.' Now that he was standing right there in front of her, though, every word she'd spoken seemed to have scattered from her head. *I'll have to re-improv!*

There was no time to stop and think, though, not when he might be distracted by his exhibit at any moment. 'Um,' Olivia said hastily, and drew a shallow breath. 'How's Lillian? Is she OK?'

'Lillian?' Charles half-frowned . . . and Olivia's heart sank as she saw his gaze pass around the room, obviously starting to catalogue his artefacts again. His lips pursed as his gaze focused on one particular candlestick nearby.

'*Lillian*, Dad?' Olivia prompted him.

'Oh, right.' Reaching for his notebook, Charles started to scribble down a note. 'Of course Lillian's OK,' he said. 'Why wouldn't she be? We've gotten over the wedding stress, and we're settling into married life in Franklin Grove.' He flipped over a new page in the notebook and kept on scribbling, sketching out what looked like a re-design of the room.

Olivia gritted her teeth. 'Maybe Lillian wants to be involved in this exhibit,' she suggested. 'It would be a good way for you to spend time together.'

'Oh, no.' Charles shook his head – and none-too-subtly re-angled himself to take a good look at the Triptych. 'Lillian's not all that interested in history,' he said. Lowering his pen for a moment, he gave Olivia a small smile. 'Plus, it's good for couples to have separate interests. You'll learn that when you're older.'

Olivia stared at her bio-dad in disbelief, forcing herself to let out her frustration in a long, rippling sigh. There was obviously no point in talking to Charles about the problem because, as far as he was concerned, there *was* no problem.

And maybe there isn't, she told herself. *Maybe I've just been over-thinking everything.*

But she didn't believe that.

Charles's gaze had already moved back to the Triptych, and Olivia gave up.

'I'll leave you to your work,' she said, forcing a smile. 'I can't wait for the exhibit this weekend.'

'Yes, yes . . .' Charles's voice followed her out of the room. 'Perhaps if I re-organised them by their *Latin* classifications . . .'

Shaking her head, Olivia fumbled her way out of the museum, past dust-covered artefacts and spooky shadows. It was a relief to step out into the fresh air, even though the sky was dark outside. As the big oak door fell shut behind her with a *boom*, the cellphone in her purse rang.

For the first time in hours, Olivia relaxed. *I know that ringtone.*

Oh, it was *so* the right time to hear Jackson's voice!

She pulled the phone out of her purse and clicked it on to see her boyfriend's very famous face fill the very tiny screen. This wasn't just a phone call – it was a video call. *Even better.* 'Hey, you!' she said. 'Can you see the creepy place I'm coming out of?' She waved the phone at the bulky museum hulking behind her in the shadows.

'Wow.' Jackson's eyebrows rose. 'Franklin Grove just keeps on getting more interesting. Are you sure you haven't snuck back on to some Hollywood set?'

'Very funny.' She rolled her eyes. 'So, how are you?'

'Well . . .' He drew a breath. 'I was actually calling because I want your advice. What do you know about the *Wanderer* trilogy?'

'Hmm.' Spotting an empty bus stop ahead, Olivia headed towards it. *I'd better sit down for this one!* Parking herself on the metal bench, she said, 'Well, I've heard of it – I mean, who *hasn't*? Those books are huge. But I've never read them.' She shrugged. 'Stories about the end of the world aren't my thing.'

'No?' Jackson frowned. 'That's interesting.' For a moment, he was silent, obviously thinking things over. Then he said, 'Amy just called me.' Amy Teller was Jackson's agent – Olivia's too, *some* of the time. 'She says that Jacob Harker's going to be producing the film version of the trilogy. He wants to know if I'm interested.'

Olivia let out a snort of pure surprise. 'Isn't the main character a guy in his mid-forties? I know you're a great actor, but I'm not sure even *you* could pull that off!'

Jackson laughed, his face breaking into the megawatt grin she'd seen on a zillion different magazine covers. 'No, I'd be playing the role of the main character's son, who dies at the very beginning – but haunts him all through the first movie.'

'Ah!' Olivia gasped with mock horror. 'Spoilers! How could you tell me that?'

'Like you were *ever* going to read a story about a war-ravaged Planet Earth stalked by hideous monsters?' Jackson teased. 'Hold on, I got another call coming in.'

Olivia waited, watching Jackson typing something on his keyboard.

Then a shadow fell over her.

Uh-oh. Olivia swivelled around in her seat and saw a girl a couple of years older than her staring at the picture on Olivia's cellphone screen. She must have been on her way to the bus stop when she'd heard Jackson speaking, and now she looked ready to pass out from sheer excitement. 'Is that really . . . *the* Jackson Caulfield . . . on your phone? Is he, like, video-calling you personally?'

Oh, no. Olivia had encountered Jackson's super-fans before. Some of them had even chased her through the streets of London when they were there filming *Eternal Sunset*! If this girl was one of them, she'd bombard Jackson with questions for the rest of the phone call – if she didn't faint right here on the pavement.

Time to go into Protective Girlfriend-mode! Let's hope Jackson keeps up.

Olivia pinned a bright smile to her face. 'Of course it's *the* Jackson Caulfield,' she said. 'But he's not *live* . . . This is a pre-recorded message. You can download it from the Jackson App. See?' She tapped the screen. 'It's on pause now.'

'Ooh. Let me see!' The girl hurried up to lean over Olivia's shoulder. 'Ohhhh. He's *so* handsome, isn't he?'

'Well . . .' Olivia gave her boyfriend a sympathetic grimace. Jackson had to keep *completely* still to keep up her story of being 'on pause'. *Thank goodness he realised what was going on in time!*

'I love his movies.' The girl sighed. 'Do you remember the bouncy castle scene in *Her Last Day*?'

'Um . . .' Olivia remembered that scene very well, but she was starting to worry that Jackson would need to blink soon!

She stood up, starting to lower the phone. 'Maybe . . .'

'Hey, wait . . .' The other girl's hand shot out to catch Olivia's wrist with an iron grip. 'Don't I know your face? Do we go to school together?'

'I don't think so,' Olivia said. She was already backing away, but she tried to keep her voice polite.

The girl gasped and pointed at her triumphantly. 'You're Olivia Abbott!'

Uh-oh. For a while, Olivia had been the main target of hate for every Jackson-fan in the universe. But there was no use denying an obvious truth, so she only smiled weakly. 'Mm-hmm.'

'Oh, you were great in *The Groves*!' The girl

beamed at her. 'I hope *Eternal Sunset* goes really well, too. Hey, could you sign my cellphone?'

'Sure.' Olivia felt the sudden tension flood out of her. *Thank goodness Jackson's fanbase isn't fuelled by jealousy any more!*

Unfortunately, in her moment of relief, she didn't notice the girl crossing the short distance between them. 'I'm Sara!' the girl said, and grabbed Olivia's hand again. 'S-A-R-A. No "H". But before you sign anything, could I see the rest of Jackson's video message? Please?'

Oh, no! Olivia tried to back away, but Sara had her hand in an unbreakable hold, her eyes gleaming eagerly as her fingers tightened around Olivia's hand. 'I just need to see him for myself, actually talking to me.'

'Oh . . . kay.' Olivia sighed, cringing inwardly. *At least I can give Jackson some prep-time, maybe.* 'All right,' she said loudly, 'you *can* see the rest of the message, but it was almost over, so it won't last that long.'

Sara frowned. 'Could you rewind it?'

'Um . . .' Olivia grinned tightly, searching for reasons. She'd improvised so much already, though, her mind had turned completely blank. *I can't think of a single reason why not*, she realised. 'OK,' she said. 'I'll rewind it by running my thumb backward on the screen, like this . . .'

It was a good thing her boyfriend was a professional actor. As guilty as Olivia felt, she was also impressed – because as she mocked rewinding via her touch-screen, Jackson did an amazing job of 'talking backwards'.

'. . . kcab ew era neht . . .'

'And here we go!' Olivia said loudly, pulling her thumb away from the screen.

'Ohhhh!' Sara gasped with delight as Jackson flashed his famous grin.

'Hi, Jackson fans,' he said. 'It's great to see you. I hope you liked the last film, and I can tell you, you'll like the new one even more. It's . . .'

'He's so amazing!' Sara moaned. She crowded in next to Olivia, almost shoving her aside. 'It's like he's talking just to me!'

Olivia sighed and stepped back as Sara hogged the screen and Jackson delivered the rest of what sounded exactly like a movie star's pre-recorded message.

Now there's someone who's really good at improv, Olivia thought. Secretly, she grinned to herself. *Next time he's in town, I will* force *him to give me some lessons!*

Chapter Seven

The next afternoon, just an hour after school had ended, Ivy hurried up the steps to the Franklin Grove Museum.

Olivia trailed behind her. 'I can't believe I'm coming back here less than twenty-four hours after my first visit,' she groaned.

'Oh, come on. It's not that bad, is it?' Ivy hammered on the door. 'Anyway, we'll get out as soon as possible.'

Ivy's eyes widened as the big oak door creaked open, revealing Albert the vampire handyman. *Wow. That jogging outfit has even more paint stains*

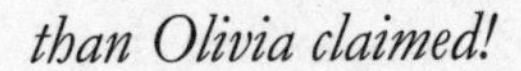

than Olivia claimed!

Albert seemed pained as he looked between them. 'The museum is not open to visitors today.'

'We know.' Ivy smiled. 'Don't worry. We're just here to see, um . . .' She winced, but remembered Olivia's story. '. . . Chas?'

Despite herself, the name came out sounding like a question. Could anyone *really* call her father by that ridiculous nickname?

Apparently, they could.

'Very well.' Sighing heavily, Albert stepped aside. 'Do you know your way?'

'I do,' Olivia said, moving forwards to take the lead as Albert disappeared off into a side room.

Ivy followed her twin through the dark, creepy halls of the old museum, until they were out of Albert's vampire earshot. 'I'll make this up to you,' she mumbled.

'I know.' Olivia gave her a faint smile, then

sidestepped just in time to avoid a massive, dust-sheet covered figure. 'OK, the main display room is just ahead.'

'Got it.' Ivy nodded firmly. 'You go distract Dad while I hunt down the vampire records room. The sooner I find out the truth about that mystery Twenty-First Law of the Night, the better for Maya *and* Brendan.'

'Are you *sure* you can find it by yourself?' Olivia asked, with a frown.

Ivy shrugged. 'The Vorld Vide Veb says it's kept in the basement of the museum. It can't be that hard to find a set of stairs leading down towards the basement, right?'

'Girls? Is that you?' Charles's voice sounded nearby, along with the echo of hurrying footsteps coming from the main display room. 'I need an opinion on my Triptych placement. I'm just not sure . . .'

Olivia winced and shooed Ivy off. 'Run,' she whispered, 'before you're trapped, too!' Then she raised her voice. 'I'm coming, Dad!'

'Don't worry,' Ivy whispered. 'I won't abandon you for long, I promise.'

Ten minutes later, though, she wasn't sure she'd be able to keep that promise. So far, all she'd found was a jumble of corridors that curved and crossed in chaotic patterns obviously designed to make sure no bunnies could accidentally stumble across the vampire records room.

Ivy would have appreciated the security a whole lot more if she didn't feel so lost! The scattered lanterns that lit the halls became fewer and fewer . . . and as she turned down another corridor, lit only by a distant lantern at the very end, she finally had to admit . . .

I'm actually scared of the dark! I really am *the worst vampire on the planet this week.*

Fighting the unease that made her want to run straight back to her twin, Ivy forced herself down the corridor. *You're doing this for Brendan*, she reminded herself.

At the very end of the corridor was a rickety-looking old door with a wrinkled, crumbling sign that read: *DANGER! KEEP OUT!*

I can't stop now. Ivy turned the handle and pulled the door open . . . revealing a pitch-black stairway that led down into a pool of shadow.

To a bunny, it might have looked like absolutely nothing was waiting downstairs. Ivy's hyper-sensitive vampire senses picked up something different in the darkness, though: the smell of books and candlelight.

Jackpot!

Ivy cautiously felt her way down the creaky wooden steps, feeling them judder underneath her feet. The darkness was so complete she had to hold out her hands on both sides to balance herself against the narrow walls. At the bottom of the staircase, she stepped forwards – and bumped straight into another door. This one wasn't rickety, though. It felt like it was made of solid, foot-thick steel, built to block out light or sound.

A moment of fumbling later, she was turning the handle and stepping into one of the most fabulous rooms she had ever seen.

Light filled the massive library, and ancient-looking stone pillars lined the walls. *Is the museum basement really this big?* Ivy wondered. *Or does the library just keep going forever underground?* She couldn't even see a far wall, only rows and rows of bookshelves receding into the distance.

Stone faces peered down watchfully from the tops of the pillars, and the smell of old books was overwhelming. Ivy wondered, if the library was this old then what was the librarian like?

Then she almost snorted. Did she really have

to ask? She knew exactly what the librarian would look like: a vampire version of Ms Milligan! Some older vampire woman with sensible shoes and a dowdy style. Oh, and glasses, definitely – *big* glasses.

Like it or not, though, Ivy still needed a librarian's help. She started towards the big mahogany desk near the front door, gasping out loud as the door behind it swung open and the librarian stepped out.

OK, this I was not *expecting!*

From his carefully styled dark hair to the crimson scarf swept around his shoulders, the black silk jacket he wore over a billowing silver blouse, and his perfectly tailored black jeans, he looked the exact opposite of how Ivy imagined librarians . . . and he also looked about twenty-five years old, at most, though Ivy knew he was probably *much* older than that.

'Really, my dear,' the librarian said, twirling a silver fountain pen between his fingers at impossible speed. 'This is against the rules. Haven't your parents explained? This library is for adult use only.'

'I know,' Ivy admitted. If it weren't for that stupid rule, she wouldn't have had to bring Olivia along to distract Charles from noticing her library visit! 'But I have something *really* important to research, and this is the only place I could think to come for answers.'

'Hmm.' The Librarian tapped the fountain pen against his lips. 'In that case . . .' He swept a flowing bow that made his long scarf flutter. 'Allow me to introduce myself. My name is Pierre.'

'I'm Ivy.' She smiled in relief. Not only was there a definite light of mischief in his eyes now, but she'd recognised the faint lilt of an accent in his voice, as faint as the hint of a Transylvanian bass in her father's voice, which told her that Pierre had probably emigrated from France a *long* time ago.

In other words, he wasn't merely older than he seemed – he was *aged*. And that meant that he was exactly the right sort of vampire to help her with her problem.

As he straightened, Pierre flashed her a grin. 'I tend not to be a stickler for the rules myself,' he murmured, 'but I'm not sure I can let a girl your age run free through my library. I don't mind you doing research down here, but you must have supervision. Agreed?'

That sounded fair to Ivy, especially since she had no idea where to even start. 'Could you help me?' she asked. 'I was hoping to find out about the Laws of the Night.'

Pierre's eyes lit up. 'Now *there's* a fascinating topic. The oldest Laws were instituted during the time of the Roman Empire, but more fascinating – in my opinion – are the amendments made over the years. They're so revealing about the true changes in vampire history!'

Uh-oh. Ivy recognised the light in Pierre's eyes. It was the same one her father got when he talked about his museum exhibit.

As Pierre launched into a freewheeling verbal history of Vampire Law, complete with footnotes and digressions, Ivy fought to keep the glazed look out of her eyes.

'. . . but, you see, to me, the deletion and reinstatement of Laws eleven, fourteen and nineteen is one of the key moments in all of vampire history!'

If I don't do something, I'll be stuck here all night, Ivy realised. *And we won't even get to the Twenty-First Law until dawn!*

Finally, as Pierre paused to draw a breath, Ivy

seized her chance. 'What do you know about the Twenty-First Law of the Night?' she blurted.

The Librarian did not hesitate. '*A vampire must never taste earthstuff when the moon is full.*'

Ivy shook her head blankly. 'Um . . . *what*?'

Pierre smiled kindly as he translated: 'Eating vegetables on a full moon.'

'*What?*' Ivy laughed. 'You have got to be pranking me.'

'Not at all, my dear.' Pierre shook his head, twirling his fountain pen idly between his fingers. 'The Law was introduced several hundred years ago, and has never been changed.'

'So . . .' Ivy could barely even say the words out loud. 'What you're telling me is that someone could be banished from their own hometown, for . . . eating a Caesar salad?'

'Well,' Pierre shrugged, his crimson scarf shifting stylishly against his shoulders. 'Vampires are known to take their Laws very seriously, no matter how silly they may seem in retrospect.' He sighed nostalgically and leaned against the desk. 'You can't have hindsight in the present, can you? If we could, I certainly would never have made that terrible mistake with the pirate and the . . .'

But Ivy didn't hear the rest of his story. She was too stunned to take it in.

How could Brendan's dad have gone along with that crazy rule when it meant kicking out his own sister? And more to the point, how many other vampires had been punished over the years for issues that were . . . well . . . *silly*?

'I'm sorry,' she said, interrupting Pierre. 'It was really great to meet you, but I have to talk to my dad. Now.'

'Then I'll wish you *au revoir*.' Pierre straightened, sweeping his scarf dramatically over his shoulder. 'But not goodbye. You are welcome to return to my library any time.'

Ivy nearly ran out of the echoing library. By the time she'd made it back to her dad's display room, she was shaking with outrage.

Charles didn't even notice as she stomped in. He was too busy lecturing Olivia, who looked glassy-eyed with hopelessness as her dad prattled on . . .

. . . and on.

'. . . But of course the *really* fascinating thing about the history of the Triptychs is –'

Balling her fists and squaring her shoulders, Ivy marched inside. 'Dad!' Her voice rapped out, cutting off her father's words. 'I need to talk to you *right now*.'

'Ivy!' Still balancing a small, three-panelled painting in his gloved hands, Charles gave her his full attention. 'What's wrong?'

'Wow,' Olivia whispered, in obvious awe. 'I really need to work on *my* Stern Voice.'

Ivy crossed her arms, focusing on her father. 'I met someone new recently,' she said. 'Someone who had a very interesting story to tell . . . about Carla Daniels.'

'*What?*' Charles gave a full-body start – and the triptych fell from his hands.

Without his vampire reflexes, it would have smashed on the marble floor. As it was, he caught it just in time. Then he walked over to the closest display case and placed it back inside with visibly trembling fingers.

'Right,' he said, turning back to his daughters. His pale face was tight, looking strained as he stripped off his gloves. He needed two attempts to get them off.

Ivy wasn't sure she'd ever seen her father so nervous – this wasn't helping her own nerves!

'We'd better all go to the break room,' he said, 'for safety's sake. I have a feeling that, if we're not careful, this conversation could cost millions of dollars' worth of damage.'

* * *

Even after they'd retreated to the staff's upstairs break room, filled with ancient couches and tables, Charles still looked as stunned as if Ivy had hit him with one of his heaviest artefacts. He handed both of the girls glasses of blood-orange juice as he joined them at a small round table, but his hands were trembling so hard the glasses clinked dangerously against the table.

'Dad?' Ivy stared at him as she took her glass. 'I don't understand. Why is this such a big deal? I mean, come on – we are talking about *vegetables*, right?'

Charles sighed as he sank down on to his chair. 'It sounds absurd now, I admit, but times were different then. Of course, I wasn't even living in Franklin Grove when it all happened, but Marc told me the story after I came here.'

Ivy traded a look with Olivia. *How many other secrets have the grown-ups been hiding from us?*

'You girls have to understand,' Charles said, 'the vampire community is a global community, with many far-flung smaller groups throughout the world. These small groups have always had to develop ways of blending in with the ordinary humans around them – but it's also been the responsibility of the Transylvanian vampires to figure out ways to watch over our kind, even from great distances. One way to do this . . . well . . .' He paused.

Fresh from her conversation with Pierre, it was easy for Ivy to fill in the blanks. 'The Laws of the Night,' she said.

Charles nodded. 'The Laws were developed to

make sure that vampires all over the world shared a common set of rules and values.'

'I understand how important safety is,' Ivy said, 'but come on. The Twenty-First Law is a bit ridiculous, don't you think? I mean, who cares whether anyone eats vegetables on a full moon?'

Charles sighed. 'I don't disagree with you,' he said. 'But you have to remember, the vampire community is rather a superstitious one. The Twenty-First Law was not set down because some vampire higher up simply had it in for veggies. It was probably based on a *genuine* belief that eating vegetables when the moon was full would bring bad luck to one's family.'

'That's . . .' Olivia began. Then she stopped, flushing.

'. . . Crazy,' Ivy finished bluntly.

Charles grimaced. 'Well, now that I'm explaining out loud, I must say that I can see that some of the Laws are quite odd by any standards. There are a couple of later amendments from the thirties that we all break every day. Perhaps they do need revising.'

Ivy snorted. '*Definitely* they need revising. I mean, after all, you and I have both broken the First Law by telling humans that vampires are *real*.'

Charles nodded. 'You're right. Perhaps I'll talk to my parents and suggest that the issue be raised in Transylvania with Queen Stefania.'

'Really?' Ivy jumped up and threw her arms around him. 'Oh, this is fantastic! Can I go to Brendan's and tell him the good news?'

'Wait!' Charles shook his head even as he patted her lightly on the back. 'Remember, this isn't "good news" yet. Even if my parents raise the issue with the Queen, it will take some time before there is any formal change to the Laws, and I can't promise –'

'I know, I know. But thank you!' Ivy gave him one last squeeze before she finally let him go.

She was practically dancing as she and Olivia left the museum five minutes later. 'I can't wait to tell Brendan!' she shouted, leaping down the steps.

Olivia giggled, poking her in the arm. 'Look at you. That last move was practically a cheerleading high-jump.'

'Bite your tongue!' Ivy scowled – for about three seconds, before her happy smile returned. Maybe Brendan's family situation couldn't be fixed immediately, but now that her dad was taking the issue all the way to the top, a happy ending was definitely possible!

Unfortunately, as soon as she approached Brendan's house, Ivy could tell that his family wasn't in a celebratory mood.

Raised voices drifted down the street – or rather, one raised voice . . . and it belonged to Marc Daniels.

'How *dare* you sneak around behind my back?' he roared.

Oh, no. Ivy raced towards the house, forcing herself to keep to a human speed instead of a full vampire blur.

If she'd needed any more proof that Mr Daniels was too angry to think straight, the sight of the front door standing ajar would have been enough. Ivy hesitated for a moment on the porch before walking inside and closing the door behind her. *I have to help!*

She found the two of them in the living room, where Mr Daniels paced through the room, red-faced and shouting.

Brendan sat slumped on the couch. 'I promise,' he said quietly. 'I didn't go looking for family secrets. I couldn't have, because I never even knew I *had* a cousin in the first place. Maya found me and told me the story.'

Ivy shifted in the doorway, and Mr Daniels' head snapped around, his face darkening. 'Were you in on this, too?'

'Mr Daniels –'

Brendan's dad didn't pause to listen. 'When you turned up last night, acting like you were going to dump my son, was that all just an act so you could help him sneak around behind my back?'

'What?' Brendan jerked around to stare at Ivy. 'You were going to *dump* me?'

'No!' Ivy gasped. *This is* exactly *why you should always knock before entering someone's house. Even if the door is already open!*

Drawing a deep breath, she turned to Mr Daniels. 'I had no idea about any of this until *after* I'd come by last night. But I've just found out about the Twenty-First Law, and I have some good news.' Her smile burst out despite the tension in the room around her. 'My dad is going to talk to his parents and see if they can't suggest to Queen Stefania that the Laws of the Night be updated to better reflect modern times.'

'Oh, wow!' Brendan jumped up. 'Ivy, that's fantastic!'

But Mr Daniels only stared at her, his eyes burning. 'What have you done?'

'What?' Ivy blurted, feeling herself stepping backwards without meaning to. 'Surely, you must want to speak to your sister again . . . don't you? I mean,' she licked her lips, trying to regain her smile, 'a Caesar salad can't be worth all this animosity, can it?'

'You have no idea what you're talking about.'

Mr Daniels swung around, turning his back on both of them. 'You don't understand the whole story.'

Brendan turned to his father. 'Then help us understand.'

Mr Daniels growled out his words without looking at either of them. 'Maybe you think the Twenty-First Law is silly, but my mother was a very superstitious vampire. Carla knew that Mother took the rules very seriously. That's why she did it, even though she didn't even *like* artichokes – and it was an artichoke, not a Caesar salad, by the way.' He shook his head. 'Carla was always rebellious, for no good reason. She broke that Law out of spite, just to show Mother she couldn't make the rules.'

Ivy winced. 'But still . . .'

'No.' Brendan's dad turned back to stare at them, his face grim. 'Do you think I'd be so stubborn that I wouldn't forgive my sister for eating an artichoke?' He clenched his hands into fists. 'No. What I couldn't forgive was that she broke that Law purely to hurt our mother – who was the best person I ever knew. And if Carla is coming back to Franklin Grove after all these years, then I know one thing . . . I won't be here to tell her to leave again.'

What? Ivy went blank with shock. Before she could think of a word to say, Mr Daniels turned and charged out of the living room.

Stunned, she and Brendan stared at each other.

'Could he really do it?' Ivy whispered. 'Would he really take you away from Franklin Grove?'

Brendan didn't answer her out loud. But she saw the horror in his eyes, and she knew – Mr Daniels was not kidding.

Ivy wrapped her arms around him, and he

buried his face in her hair. 'It's going to be all right,' she whispered.

But secretly, she thought: *This is a total disaster.*

Chapter Eight

Olivia looked around the dinner table the next night and sighed. *This is the oddest dinner I've ever had at my bio-dad's house . . . and that's really saying something!*

When she'd stopped by the house that evening, she'd hoped to grab a private moment with her stepmom to finally figure out what was going on. She'd arrived just as dinner was ready, though, so now there were four people sitting at the dining table . . . and three of them seemed to be in another world entirely.

Charles had a notepad open in his lap, which

he never looked away from even as he forked steak into his mouth. Ivy looked glum as she picked at her sweet potato, obviously lost in her worries over Brendan. Lillian – who looked dressed for a royal banquet, rather than an ordinary dinner at home – seemed to have no appetite at all.

Weirder still, Lillian's smartphone chirped in her handbag every few minutes. Charles didn't even notice, and Lillian never moved to answer it – but her perfectly made-up face twitched every time it made a noise.

I can't take this any more. It wasn't just curiosity or nosiness for Olivia now. If someone didn't tell her what was going on soon, she might *actually* explode!

Taking a deep breath, she set down her salad fork. 'Lillian,' she said. 'How was your day?'

'What?' Lillian blinked, her mascaraed

eyelashes dark against her pale skin. One hand moved to fidget with the emerald necklace around her neck. 'Oh. Ah. Fine.'

Then she went straight back to pushing her uneaten steak around her plate, gold-and-silver bracelets rattling against each other on her wrist.

Time for Plan B: make Lillian and Charles talk to each other!

'So, Dad,' Olivia said brightly. 'Has Lillian been to the museum yet? What did she think of the exhibit?'

'Mmm?' Charles didn't even look up from his notepad, where he was busily scribbling notes even as he continued to eat.

Lillian's words came out in a mumble. 'Looking forward to Saturday, just like everyone else.'

Olivia forced extra peppiness into her smile. 'But aren't you impatient? Don't you want a sneak peek?'

Lillian didn't even look up. 'I hate spoilers.'

Drat. Olivia's shoulders slumped. A dinner table with a fabulous meal was just *not* the right setting for any kind of confrontation.

'Sorry. Did you ask me a question, Olivia?' Charles shook himself, as if he were shaking off a trance. 'This is very rude of me, isn't it?' He grimaced as he held up his notepad. 'I beg your pardon, everyone. Why don't I take my food into my study so I can get some more work done without being impolite?'

'Dad . . .' Olivia rolled her eyes. 'I saw the museum yesterday, remember? I think you're done! Seriously, it looks as good as it needs to. Doesn't it, Ivy?'

'Wha–?' Ivy's voice sounded bleary. Clearly, she had *no* idea what the others had been talking about.

'Ivy agrees,' Olivia said firmly to their father.

'You've done a great job, so stop worrying about it!'

'Why, thank you, Olivia.' Charles smiled at her. 'I appreciate the kind words. However, this isn't about this weekend's exhibit. It's about what I might do with the South Wing of the museum if it is, indeed, entrusted to me afterwards.'

'What?' Olivia stared at him. 'But you've been working so hard on the exhibit. Can't you give yourself a little break?' *Or some time to pay attention to your wife?* she added silently. *Can't you see how weird Lillian's acting?*

But Charles was already standing up. 'I'm afraid not, my dear. There's no time to be lost. I want to do something spectacular – but more than that, it needs to be *worthwhile*.'

He headed out of the room, leaving Olivia staring helplessly after him. At the table, Ivy was still busy using her fork to turn her sweet potato into mangled, not-so-sweet mashed potato, while Lillian seemed to have turned into stone.

As Olivia watched Charles disappear through the door, irritation flashed through her, tightening her chest. *How can such a smart man be so oblivious to how his own family feels right now?*

Looking again at Lillian's mask-like face, where all expression had been carefully hidden, Olivia released her tension in a sigh.

'I like your dress, Lillian,' Olivia offered. 'It's very . . .' *Formal*, she finished in her head. Who wore a black silk evening gown to a family dinner at home? '. . . elegant,' she finished out loud. 'Where did you –?'

'Sorry!' Lillian's head whipped to the side as her smartphone chirped yet again. She lunged for her handbag. 'Excuse me. I just have to see who's trying to contact me – they seem rather *insistent*.'

'OK,' Olivia said. But she frowned as she saw

Lillian race upstairs with full vampiric speed, obviously waiting to answer the phone until she was out of hearing range of everyone else. *Why would she need that much privacy for her call, if she doesn't even know who's trying to talk to her?*

'Oh.' Ivy sighed, emerging for the first time from her distraction. 'That reminds me, I left my phone in my room. Brendan might need to call me. Maybe . . .'

'I'll get it for you,' Olivia said. She gave a mock-serious face, pointing to the mangled mess on Ivy's plate. 'Just promise me you'll put that poor food out of its misery!'

'Will do.' Ivy gave her a sad half-smile and a mock salute.

Olivia started up the stairs towards her sister's room. As she walked past Charles and Lillian's bedroom door, though, the sound of Lillian's strained, unhappy voice stopped her in her tracks.

'I'm really, really not sure about this,' Lillian said softly.

'Are you nuts?' The crackly voice of Jacob Harker sounded through the phone so loudly that even Olivia could hear it in the hallway outside. 'You would have to be, like, totally crazy to turn this down! It'll give your career a *massive* boost.'

'I know,' Lillian said, 'but –'

'This director *really* wants you on the project. To prove it, he's offered to produce your feature-length directorial debut after you wrap. He just wants you to help him out on this one shoot.'

There was a long, agonising pause. Olivia could almost feel her stepmom's indecision vibrating through the air. She held her breath to keep from making any tell-tale noises.

But why is this such a hard decision? Olivia wondered. *Why would she be so unsure about taking a new job on a movie?* Yes, Lillian had moved to

Franklin Grove, but she and Charles must have factored in that she would need to travel from time to time. After all, it was her movie career that had brought her to Franklin Grove in the first place, at the beginning of the year.

Finally, Lillian let out a heavy sigh. 'I'll think about it,' she told Harker. 'Now *come in, please.*'

What? Olivia's eyebrows rose. Why would Lillian ask Jacob Harker – who was in another state – to come into the room?

. . . *Oh, wait. She didn't ask Harker. Oops!*

Olivia winced. After all the times the vampires around her had been caught off-guard in this past week, why did tonight have to be the night Lillian started hearing like a vampire again?

Bracing herself, Olivia opened the door.

Inside the bedroom, Lillian stood by a plush, ornate double-coffin in the shape of a heart. As Olivia stepped inside, Lillian placed her smartphone on the glossy wooden lid of the coffin and turned to give her stepdaughter a stern look.

'Eavesdropping is never nice, Olivia. You're old enough to know that by now.'

'I'm sorry!' Olivia rushed forwards across the thick, dark carpet. 'I really didn't mean to, but I couldn't help it. *Please* don't think of it as a betrayal! I just . . .' She bit her lip, faltering just as she reached her stepmom's side. 'I got it in my head that you were getting ready to run away from Franklin Grove or something.'

Lillian stared at her. 'Whatever gave you that idea?'

Olivia twisted her hands together. 'I saw you,' she whispered, 'in the supermarket, picking up a travel guide. And you've not been yourself lately – it's like you're trying too hard to *prove* that you like Franklin Grove and you fit in here.'

'Olivia . . .' Lillian began.

Olivia couldn't stop herself. 'You're trying too hard,' she said, looking from her stepmother's elaborately upswept hair to her evening gown and rich garnet necklace. 'You've been trying so hard to convince *someone* that everything's OK, that it's becoming so obvious everything's *not* OK.'

Lillian looked at her for a long moment without speaking. Then, slowly, she smiled. 'Gosh, I didn't think it would take you such a short time to be able to read my moods so well,' she said. 'If I'm not careful, you and Ivy are going to be able to twist me round your little fingers!'

Olivia laughed and walked across the room to her stepmom, wrapping her in a hug. 'I'm right here if you need to talk,' she promised.

Lillian raised her eyebrows thoughtfully. 'OK,' she said. 'I'd like that. But . . .' She flipped open the coffin and climbed inside, carefully arranging the skirts of her silk evening gown against the rich crimson velvet of the coffin's lining. 'I'm going to need to be really relaxed for *this* conversation.'

Olivia blinked. 'OK.' *I can deal with this*, she told herself. After all, she'd finally gotten Lillian to start talking. She could totally handle talking to someone while they lay down inside a coffin!

As Lillian got comfortable, the lines of tension in her face eased away. For the first time all week, she actually looked genuinely peaceful. When she started to speak, her voice was quiet.

'I wasn't planning to leave,' she said. 'I was looking at travel guides because I was trying to find out how easy it would be to fly back and forth from the *Wanderer* location shoot to Franklin Grove.'

'*Wanderer*? I've heard about that movie!' Olivia grabbed the coffin edge in her excitement – then let go. *Too weird!* Backing away from the coffin, she continued: 'Mr Harker asked Jackson if he wanted to act in it.'

'Really?' Lillian seemed to ponder that for a moment. 'Well, Jackson would be excellent as the main character's son. Is he going to do it?'

'I don't know,' Olivia said, 'but that's not important. What matters right now is, why are you *not* doing it?'

Lillian sighed, shifting her head against her crimson cushion. 'It turns out that it wouldn't be easy at all to fly back and forth from the shoot to Franklin Grove. It's a post-apocalyptic movie, set largely in the desert. That means location work, mostly in Africa.'

'Oh.' Frowning, Olivia nibbled on her lower lip. 'OK, so you wouldn't be coming back every weekend. But it's one shoot – four or five months at the most, right? So . . . if the director wants to help you make your own movie afterwards, it might be worth it.'

Lillian sighed again and closed her eyes. This time, Olivia had to look away. Lying inside the coffin with her eyes shut, Olivia's stepmom looked achingly beautiful and ethereal, but also quite . . . *dead.* Olivia swallowed hard. *This is the hardest part of vampire culture to deal with!*

When Lillian spoke again, though, her words startled Olivia out of her discomfort. 'It *is* just one movie shoot,' Lillian said, 'but Harker wants to film all three movies back-to-back . . . over a period of eighteen months.'

Olivia gasped. *Eighteen months?* Taking that job really would mean Lillian effectively moving away!

'Of course I can't do it,' Lillian said. 'I couldn't bear to spend that long away from my new family – and I would never want Charles to have to relocate Ivy and separate you two girls again.'

'Nooo . . .' Olivia trailed the word out unhappily.

'Olivia?' Ivy's voice called up from downstairs. 'I've destroyed my sweet potato, like, five times while waiting. Do you need *help* looking for my phone?'

'No, I'm fine,' Olivia called back. 'I'll be right down.'

She bit her lip, turning back to her stepmom. The thought of losing Ivy for a year and a half was unbearable, but it was *so* unfair that Lillian's ambitions couldn't match up with her new life in Franklin Grove!

Lillian suddenly sat up in the coffin, reaching out for Olivia. Olivia had to look away sharply. *This is way too much of a horror movie moment!*

Her stepmom's touch was gentle, though, as she took Olivia's hand. 'I promise,' Lillian said, 'that it's not Franklin Grove making me unhappy.

I can't tell you how happy I am being married to Charles – and how thrilled I am that I get to be stepmother to the two coolest teenagers I've ever known.'

Olivia squeezed her stepmom's hand, feeling the gentle sting of tears in her eyes. 'We're really thrilled about that, too,' she said.

Lillian's expression turned wistful. 'I just wish I could be creative here, that's all. That's the only reason I even considered taking the *Wanderer* job – because there's not much creative outlet in Franklin Grove.'

Olivia gave a hiccupy laugh. 'I've heard that before,' she said, 'from Camilla.'

Her friend had always said that Franklin Grove wasn't cinematic. In fact, Camilla would probably tell Lillian that herself, if she ever worked up the nerve to speak to her. Maybe at the exhibit on Saturday . . .

That's it!

Too excited to be creeped out, Olivia reached right into the coffin to give her stepmom a big hug.

'Whoa! What was that for?' Lillian asked, laughing.

Olivia grinned with delight as she bounced back up and headed for the door. 'I can't explain right now, but I'm getting an idea!'

'What kind of idea?' Lillian called after her.

But Olivia was already hurrying out of the room. 'If it's a good one,' she called back over her shoulder, 'you'll find out all about it . . . on Saturday!'

Chapter Nine

Ivy felt Brendan's hand tighten around hers as the Lincoln Vale mall rose before them, glass-walled and impressive.

Ivy pointed at Maya, standing just by the entrance. 'There she is.'

'Come on,' said Maya, hurrying towards them. 'Let's not go inside. There's someone I want you to meet.'

Ivy and Brendan followed her down the street to a small, family-style diner half a block away. The décor was quiet, cosy and completely unsuited to the glamorous woman who sat at a table near the back. Her long black hair rippled down the back of her stylish black trouser suit, an elegant gold choker surrounded her slim neck . . . and even with contact lenses disguising her real eye colour, her resemblance to Maya was unmistakable.

She might look just the right age to have a daughter in high school, but she had to be at least one hundred years old . . . and she was Brendan's aunt.

'Oh!' She gasped, raising one hand to her throat as she rose to greet them. Her gaze went straight to Brendan. 'Are you really my nephew?'

'This is Brendan, Mom,' Maya said.

'I can't believe it!' Carla wrapped her arms around him. 'It is so amazing to finally meet you!'

Brendan patted her back awkwardly. 'Um . . . you, too.'

Carla's eyes glistened with unshed tears as

she pulled him down to sit with her at the table. 'This is awful,' she said. 'I don't know anything about you – what you like, what you don't . . .' She swiped at her eyes and smiled brilliantly. 'But I promise: if you write out a list, I will buy you gifts for every missed birthday and Christmas!'

Brendan laughed, visibly relaxing. 'That's really not necessary. Getting long-lost family is enough of a gift.'

Carla pressed her lips together for a moment, obviously filled with emotion. 'It's like looking at my brother a hundred years ago,' she whispered at last.

'Whoa.' Brendan whipped his head around, his eyes darting around the room. 'We need to be careful about saying things like that in public.'

'Of course.' Carla gave a guilty smile. 'It's funny – since I haven't had any of *our kind* around day after day, I've found it much easier not to let anything slip, because I don't normally *have* these conversations any more!' She sighed, sitting back in her chair as Maya and Ivy took their own places at the table. 'That's something our community doesn't really take into account – that maybe, we get *too* comfortable among our own company.

'Not that I don't miss it.' Her smile drooped. 'I really, really do.'

Ivy felt a wave of sympathy as she saw the loneliness in Carla's eyes. She couldn't even imagine being parted from Olivia for so long.

Then she tuned back into the conversation and stiffened.

'. . . but of course there's no point talking to those hoity-toity Transylvanians who only care about the "rules"!' She scowled. 'Trust me, I could do without *their* kind forever!'

Ivy took a deep breath, forcing herself not to

take offence. As she looked down at the table, Maya cleared her throat.

'Um, Mom?' she whispered. 'Ivy's family are actually *from* a highborn Transylvanian bloodline.'

'Really?' For the first time, Carla looked directly at Ivy. Recognition passed over her face. 'Oh, of course! I can see it in your bone structure now. You're a Lazar, aren't you?'

Ivy shrugged awkwardly. 'Yup.'

'Ohhhh . . .' Carla's face lit up with interest. 'You must be one of the twins who were profiled in *VAMP* magazine! I still have my subscription – it's about the only part of my identity that *wasn't* taken away from me.'

The bitterness disappeared from her voice, though, as she leaned forwards. 'Yes, of course. You're the daughter of a vampire father . . . who broke an older, far more serious rule than I ever did.'

'That's right.' Taking Carla's hand, Ivy met her gaze full-on. 'I know it's not fair,' she said, 'and I'm here to help in any way I can.'

She opened her mouth to say more, then stopped, biting her lip. If she mentioned that her dad was planning to talk to his royal connections, she might get Carla's hopes up . . . and if anything went wrong, Brendan's aunt would be crushed.

Carla sighed, sliding her hand away. 'I'm sorry for what I said before,' she said. 'This whole situation has just made me really emotional. Being so close to Franklin Grove, after so long away . . . well, I'm homesick.'

'That's OK.' Ivy smiled reassuringly. 'I know a little bit about how that feels.' Just the memory of her time at the snooty Wallachia Academy, so far away from her family and friends, made her wince.

Carla caught the movement. 'Oh?' She cocked her head. 'When were you sent away?'

'It's . . . a long story, for another time.' Ivy looked over Carla's head at the service door of the diner, which was just swinging open. 'And look, here comes the waitress.'

All four vampires went silent as the smiling waitress approached. 'How can I help you folks today?'

'Ah,' Carla picked up a menu. 'I'll have a steak, please. Extra rare.'

'Sounds good, ma'am. Now, would you prefer that with potatoes or artichokes?' The waitress waited expectantly, her pen hovering above her notepad.

As everyone else turned to look at her, Carla gave a tight smile. 'Potatoes,' she said. 'Trust me. I'm allergic to artichokes.'

An hour and a half later, Ivy was walking hand-in-hand with Brendan down his street, heading towards the Daniels house without any hurry. As Brendan swung her hand in his, he looked more relaxed than she'd seen him in days.

'Well, that went a lot better than I was expecting.' He grinned, his dark hair falling over his forehead. 'Although, I could definitely see in Aunt Carla the same stubbornness that I've seen in my dad this week. They are *so* related!'

'Absolutely.' Ivy sighed. 'I hope we can figure things out for them soon. Ever since I got a sister of my own, I've *never* been able to understand how siblings could ever fall out. It must be miserable for both of them.'

'Yeah.' Brendan echoed her sigh as they came to a halt in front of his house. 'Well . . . here goes.'

Ivy squeezed his hand. 'Do you want me to come in with you? If your dad's still angry, it might be good for you guys to have company, to give him some time to cool off.'

'Ivy Vega, you are the best.' Brendan pulled her in for a warm hug. 'I would love for you to hang out for a bit,' he whispered into her hair, 'but you don't have to worry about my dad. He seemed pretty calm this morning.'

But when they stepped inside a moment later, the house looked as if it had been turned inside-out. *Uh-oh*, Ivy thought, as she looked at the books and papers scattered around the living room. *What's going on?*

Loud clattering noises sounded in the next room, along with the sound of a busy printer in the office. Brendan's dad swept into the living room a minute later, his arms full of maps and guidebooks. 'Brendan! Ivy!' he said warmly. 'What do you two know about a town called Pine Wood?'

'Um . . .?' Ivy shrugged. It rang a *vague* bell, but –

Brendan frowned. 'Wasn't there a girl from Franklin Grove who moved there over the summer? Debi something?'

'That's right!' Ivy said. 'She was a cheerleader – Olivia would know.' *Aha!* Now she remembered. 'Actually, Olivia's going to do some filming there just before Thanksgiving!'

Brendan frowned. 'But, Dad, why are you asking?' As he looked at his dad, suspicion gathered on his face.

Before Marc Daniels could say a word, a loud ringing sounded from the computer in the study.

'Here, take these!' Mr Daniels bundled the maps and guidebooks into Brendan's hands. 'I have to answer this call!'

Juggling his armful, Brendan followed straight after his dad. Ivy followed Brendan into the small study, where even more maps were being printed as they entered.

A video-messaging programme was blinking in alert on the computer screen, and the ID on the caller read: *Boss-Man.*

Ivy raised her eyebrows at Brendan as the two of them stepped back, out of sight.

'Dad's boss,' Brendan whispered.

Then they both went silent as the call clicked on.

On the screen, a hearty-looking, silver-haired man nearly bellowed his words. 'Daniels! Have you thought any more about my suggestion? You know I need an answer soon!'

Mr Daniels smiled broadly. 'I'm thinking about it,' he said, 'and in fact, I'm doing a bit of research about Pine Wood right now.'

Oh, no!

Ivy and Brendan shared a look of equal horror. So much for trying to fix things between Mr Daniels and his sister!

Was he actually thinking of following through on his threat to *move away*, just in case Carla ever moved back to town?

Dread tingled in Ivy's chest as she looked into her boyfriend's face.

Too many people threaten to leave Franklin Grove. It needs to stop – right now!

Chapter Ten

As Olivia walked towards the Franklin Grove Museum that Saturday, she shook her head in wonder.

Wow. Dad really pulled it off!

A long, snaking line of visitors stretched all the way out to the street, waiting their turn to come in. The small groups of people who'd already seen the exhibit looked almost giddy as they walked back out of the building.

One man stopped to yell back to the whole line of waiting visitors. 'Don't give up. That display is magical. Those artefacts . . .' He shook his head, looking almost tearful. 'I've never seen anything like them. Charles Vega is a *genius*!'

Oh, really? Olivia raised her eyebrows as she walked around the museum to the side-entrance reserved for special guests – or in other words, for vampires (and their bunny relatives!). The brisk October air rustled through her gauzy pink cashmere shrug and the darker rose-pink silk wrap dress she wore underneath. Olivia sighed as she thought back to the museum visitor's words. She was proud of her bio-dad, but she had to admit, he really hadn't been acting all that smart this week. Would a *real* genius completely fail to notice the problems his new wife was having?

She was so absorbed in her thoughts that she almost walked straight into the girl heading towards her. 'Oh!' She caught herself just in time. 'I'm so s– oh, *Camilla*!' Olivia felt her face break into a beaming smile as she took in the sight of her best friend. 'I'm so glad you're here!'

'Do I look OK?' Camilla fingered one bouncy blonde curl, fidgeting nervously. 'I wanted to look artistic – but not full of myself, you know? And it had to be fancy, but –'

'You look perfect,' Olivia assured her.

It was true. From the garnet brooch pinned to her velvet black beret to the black-and-white silk Charlie Chaplin outfit she wore, Camilla had definitely dressed up. But she was just as definitely still her artistic self.

'Now, come on.' Olivia took her friend's arm. 'I promise, I'll answer *all* your questions about last week's block of filming – but first, we have a mission.'

'Really?' Camilla brightened. 'Hey, do you think you could get me in through the secret "family entrance"? That bouncer looks pretty scary.'

'Hmm.' Olivia looked at the side-entrance,

where Albert – wearing a tuxedo, rather than his paint-stained jogging outfit – stood with his arms crossed, looking as if he'd swallowed a lemon. 'It's worth a try,' she decided. 'Let's do it!'

. . . *And let's hope I don't get into trouble for this!* she added silently.

As they neared the door, Olivia pasted on a big smile. She was already preparing her rationalisation as she opened her mouth . . .

. . . but she didn't have time to deliver it. Albert was already stepping back and opening the door. 'This Camilla?' he grunted.

'Um, yes,' Camilla said, and traded a wide-eyed glance with Olivia.

Albert nodded. 'Lillian told me to expect her as well.'

Phew. Olivia beamed at him as they swept past into the museum. *How perfect!* She'd gotten out of this one without having to lie *or* put the vampire secret at risk. And best of all, she'd gotten Camilla inside, exactly where she needed her.

Whether Camilla knew it or not, she was *essential* to Olivia's plan to fix everything that was wrong with her family!

Ivy traded a nervous look with Brendan behind Marc Daniels's back as they led him around the museum exhibit.

'*Let's hope this works!*' Brendan mouthed silently to her.

Ivy could only nod . . . then fix a quick smile on her face as Mr Daniels turned around. 'Isn't it wonderful?' she asked.

'It really is.' Brendan's dad had been in a dark mood for days, but the exhibit was working its magic on him. At last, some of the scowl lines were easing from his forehead. 'Your father has done an amazing job, Ivy. This whole exhibit is gorgeous.' He sighed. 'It's such a rich history that our kind has. I forget that sometimes.'

'You have to see this next piece.' Forcing herself to move as if this really were nothing more than a casual wander, Ivy led him to a velvet cushion around the next corner.

On top of the jet-black cushion lay a long, swirling piece of gold jewellery studded with deep-set, glinting gemstones, from white, black and yellow diamonds to pigeon-blood rubies. Two golden serpents lay ensnared, apparently as a single piece . . . but in actuality, as the chart in the back of the glass case showed, the two serpents came apart at a single twist. Then, the yellow-gold serpent would form a bracelet while the white-gold serpent became an ornate ring.

'The Jewellery of the Two Sisters,' Mr Daniels breathed. He reached out as if to touch the glass case, and visibly stopped himself just in time. 'I can't believe I'm really seeing it with my own eyes.'

Brendan coughed. 'So . . . you've heard of it before?'

His father couldn't seem to look away from the ensnared serpents. 'I've heard the legend,' he replied. 'It's said that these pieces originally belonged to two va– that is, *V* sisters. The serpents represent the two qualities that are most important to any of our kind – discretion and power.'

He drew a deep, reverent breath, and dropped his voice to a thread-like whisper that only another vampire could hear. 'Almost a thousand years ago, the two sisters were sent away on a vampire crusade. They divided the two pieces between them as a symbol of their desire to one day find each other. But only one sister returned with her half of the jewellery. The other sister was never found. And according to legend, her ring was left discarded beneath a pile of crumbling stone.'

Sniffing, he dropped his head. 'Sorry.' He shook his head, keeping his eyes averted. 'That story has always got to me, every time I've heard it. And to actually see the pieces now, making it all so real . . .'

'Of course,' Ivy murmured.

It got to her, too. How could it not? The idea of being separated from Olivia forever . . . it was unbearable.

And to think, just over a year ago, I still thought I was an only child! Ivy gave a rueful smile. *I am so thankful to have been proved wrong on that.*

But that wasn't – *couldn't* be – her main concern. Right now, she just had one big question . . . the same question she could see in Brendan's eyes:

Would Mr Daniels's spontaneous monologue soften him up for the surprise they'd prepared?

Or was everything about to explode in their faces?

'I've always loved that story, too.' Carla spoke behind them, her voice soft. As Mr Daniels spun around to face her, she smiled tentatively. 'Ever since our father first sat us down and told it to us. Do you remember? It was on a steam-train journey to California.'

But Marc Daniels still hadn't said a word. He was staring at his sister, his face completely unreadable. Ivy shot a quick, questioning look at Brendan – who only shrugged, looking just as baffled as she felt. Was his dad outraged? Too furious to speak? Or . . .?

The chiming sound of a fork tapping a glass filtered through the noise of the crowd, making everyone fall silent.

'May I have everyone's attention?' Charles Vega stood in the centre of the room, smiling broadly. 'I'd like to give my most sincere thanks to all of you for making the effort to visit the museum today. I hope you'll all put the word out so that everyone in Franklin Grove knows we have no need to leave town to experience a bit of majestic culture. We draw quite a lot of culture and wonder to our own community, right here – because this is a magical place, without a doubt.'

As the crowd began to clap, Charles inclined his head graciously, but then he held up his hand for silence. 'These artefacts on display,' he said, 'are not just motionless pieces of clay or gold and silver, brass and stone. They are *alive* – alive with the history that they have seen and the history that they remember. Through them, *we* might remember it, too.'

His gaze passed over the crowd. 'History teaches us many vital lessons, often different ones each time. Perhaps the most important lesson, though, is that history is just that . . . *history*. The past is the past, and we can only remember it – sometimes fondly, sometimes not. But, whether those memories be positive or negative, we can always learn from them. In fact, we *must* learn from them – because . . .' his voice deepened, echoing around the spellbound room, '. . . our history shapes our hopes for *tomorrow*.'

The room erupted into applause, and warm pride rose in Ivy. *Just look at my dad!*

Charles wasn't the stressed-out, panicky panicker he'd been all week. Now, he was back to being the charming, confident man Ivy had grown up knowing – except, he was using the kind of grand, airy and vague language that she usually only heard from Olivia's adoptive dad!

Ivy grinned at the thought, but it didn't diminish her pride. There was absolutely no doubt that Charles had meant every word he'd said . . .

. . . And Marc Daniels obviously *felt* it, from the deep, raw emotions running across his face.

'A toast!' Charles called. 'To everybody at this museum!'

Carla Daniels's lips wobbled. She hadn't looked away from her brother for an instant. 'Everybody?' she whispered. 'Marc?'

Brendan's dad looked at her and shook his head wordlessly.

Oh, no! Panic almost choked Ivy. *It didn't work?*

Then Brendan's dad lunged forwards to wrap his sister in an enormous hug. He looked as if he might never let her go.

Ivy felt her eyes well up even as Brendan grabbed her hand and squeezed it hard. Across the room, she could see Maya gazing, spellbound, at the sight. Ivy might be forcing back her own happy tears, but Maya wasn't even trying – her tears slipped freely down her face as her lips curved into a joyous grin.

Ivy tucked her head into her boyfriend's shoulder and sighed happily as she watched the reunion before her.

No wonder Olivia enjoys meddling so much!

The sky outside the long museum windows was already darkening by the time the exhibit finally started to wind down. As Olivia watched, a long line of patrons filed past Charles, taking turns just to shake his hand. *He really is the king of the hour*, she thought affectionately, as their praises filled the air.

'What a marvellous exhibition that was!'

'There's been nothing like it here before.'

'Amazing!'

'Come on,' Olivia whispered to Camilla, as

she grabbed her friend's hand to pull her through the crowd.

But Lillian beat them to her bio-dad. 'Congratulations, Charles,' she said, giving him a warm embrace. 'This really is even more impressive than I'd expected.'

'Thank you, darling.' Charles smiled at her. 'I just wish I could figure out exactly what to do with the South Wing next.'

Aha! Olivia cleared her throat, stepping forwards while Camilla hung behind. 'Dad, didn't you mention before that you didn't think there should be any more space devoted to artefacts? I'm sure you said' – *in one of your loooong monologues earlier this week!* – 'that the existing wings gave more than enough room for exhibitions already.'

'Well, yes.' Charles sighed. 'But what else can be done in a museum?'

'Well . . .' Olivia straightened her shoulders,

running through the speech she had been practising – this was no time for improv! 'Isn't the South Wing really just a big empty space right now?' She gave him a meaningful look. 'It doesn't *look* like a museum . . . so, therefore, can it really be *called* a museum?'

Her adoptive dad would surely have been proud of her making such a vague – but very important-sounding – statement!

Charles frowned. 'I suppose you have a point,' he said. 'But, my dear daughter, I'm a bit of a traditionalist. I hardly think it would be appropriate to turn a former museum wing into a diner, or whatever it is that you might be suggesting.'

Olivia laughed as she took her bio-dad's arm. 'That's not what I was thinking at all. Just tell me . . .' She narrowed her eyes as she launched into the question she'd prepared. 'What *is* a museum for? The first thing that comes into your mind.'

But she couldn't help the way her hand tightened on his arm with nerves as she waited for his answer. *Oh, please let me know my bio-dad – and my stepmom – well enough to be right about this!*

Charles raised his eyebrows. 'The first thing that comes into my mind . . . art!'

Yes!

Olivia did silent cheers as he continued: 'A museum is a house of art – the finest art of yesterday.'

'Mm-hmm.' With an effort, Olivia kept her voice calm. 'But is that all?'

Lillian jumped in, just as Olivia had hoped she would. 'A museum is a *record* of art – all kinds of art, from all different points in time.' She smiled fondly at her husband. 'Charles said it himself, in his inspiring speech – our history shapes our *tomorrow*.'

'Exactly!' Olivia couldn't help bouncing on her toes, despite her sparkly kitten heels. 'So . . . is there any reason the South Wing of this museum can't be a house of *tomorrow's* art?'

'Hmm.' Charles narrowed his eyes as he looked down at her, amusement and curiosity mingling in his expression. 'How exactly do you plan to pull that off? Without going for a joyride in a time machine, that is.'

Olivia looked to Lillian. 'What do *you* think?'

'Well, what if . . .' Lillian's face lit up with gathering excitement. 'Oh, *yes!* Charles, what if you converted the South Wing into a *Creative Space* for local artists? A workshop where talented, young, local people could be creative in a relaxed environment?'

Please, please, please say yes! Olivia urged her father silently.

For a long moment, Charles was silent, his face

furrowed in thought. Then a smile spread across his face. 'What an absolutely perfect idea. But we would need someone to run it. Who would be good at *that*? Hmm . . .'

'Good question,' Olivia said brightly, using every bit of her dramatic training to keep her expression blank as Lillian gave a visible twitch of frustration. '*Who* could possibly run that workshop?'

'Well . . .' Charles rubbed his jaw thoughtfully, apparently thinking out loud. 'Who do we know who's smart, talented, creative *and* responsible . . . not to mention good with young people? Now, that's a real puzzler.'

Oh, come on. Olivia stared at him. In the corner of her eye, she could see her stepmom's face turning utterly expressionless. Lillian was clearly having to work hard to hide her own feelings right now, but she shouldn't have had to.

Is my bio-dad really that *dense?* Olivia wondered.

Then Charles's face broke into a grin, and Olivia realised that he'd been joking the whole time.

'Oh, come now,' he said. 'We all know the answer, don't we?' He turned to Lillian. 'Who could possibly be better than you, darling? And not only that – the two of us could collaborate on the design for the space!'

Lillian's face broke into a beaming smile. 'I'm having so many ideas for what we could do! The films we could make, the screenings we could put on – of course we'd have to have a Local Film Group, where movie nuts could talk all day about films . . .'

Behind Olivia, Camilla let out an excited yelp at all the movie talk.

The sound made Lillian turn around with a quick smile. 'Camilla, I assume you're in? I don't think I could do this without a helper.'

'*Yes!*' Camilla almost knocked Olivia over as she barged past to clutch hands with Lillian. Suddenly, words were spilling out of her, breaking through all the shyness that had held her silent until then. 'I have been so desperate for a place where I could be creative *with structure*!'

Lillian nodded firmly. 'I want to hear *all* of your ideas. Come find a quiet corner with me, and we'll brainstorm.'

She started to pull Camilla away . . . then paused to pull out the cellphone from her handbag. 'I just have to call someone first . . .'

She's calling Harker to turn down his offer, Olivia realised, with a bittersweet pang. She knew exactly how that kind of phone call went.

Where was Jackson right now? And how long would it be before they were really together again, for more than a scattered week here or there?

Olivia sighed.

She hated that Lillian had to turn down this opportunity . . . but a talented filmmaker like Lillian would always get new opportunities in the future. Olivia was sure of that.

As her bio-dad turned back to receive the congratulations of the crowd, Olivia felt a familiar hand curve around her arm. Ivy stood behind her, holding hands with Brendan and beaming.

'We heard it all,' Ivy said. 'Everyone's making incredible plans for the future, huh?'

'Including my dad and Aunt Carla,' Brendan said, and shook his head in wonder. 'And we're not moving to Pine Wood.'

'I'm so glad!' Olivia reached out to grab his free hand and Ivy's at the same time. 'Well, we all knew this exhibit would be a hit, didn't we?'

'Always,' Ivy said. 'But I have to say, as much as I admire Dad . . .' She shook her head, grinning. 'Even I wasn't expecting such a fabulous outcome!'

'How could you not, when we were *both* involved?' Beaming, Olivia released Brendan's hand to wrap him and her sister in a group hug. Together, they'd found a way to keep everyone they loved exactly where they belonged . . . here in Franklin Grove, with them.

And now that everything was all settled . . .

'It's time to solve a new mystery,' Olivia whispered to her twin. 'Because I can't wait another minute to start looking for those vintage fashions hidden *somewhere* in this museum!'

Ivy laughed. Brendan groaned. But there was no question in Olivia's mind that they would find the hidden fashions together . . . because when she was with her twin sister, *nothing* was impossible.

FROM: Reiko@banpmail.com
TO: I-V@vvv.com
SUBJECT: Visiting!

Hi Ivy! I'm sure you've heard by now that Sophia is going to be on an exchange programme, and will be visiting Tokyo for two weeks. I am the student who will be swapping places with her! My name is Reiko, and I am so excited! I've never been to America before.

I've been emailing Sophia ever since our schools told us about the exchange, and she has told me lots about you – you sound like the coolest girl, and I can't wait to meet up. I hope we have time to hang out when I'm in Franklin Grove! What sorts of things do you like to do in your spare time?

I like sports – which I've always played, ever since I was very small.

I started with soccer and I still love it, but it's hard to play with non-vamps. Especially boys – they HATE IT when any girl is stronger and faster than them. Although, I must admit, I do like to watch them sulk after I outsprint them – or try not to cry after I've knocked them to the ground! Now I play tennis mostly – as you can imagine, I am the undefeated REIGNING CHAMPION at my school!

But that is why I'm so very excited to visit America – all the sports! You must go to games all the time, right? Basketball, baseball, soccer – so much choice! You MUST take me to a game with you – I will watch anything! And if there aren't any games on, maybe we can have one of our

own? I'm bringing my tennis racket, because Sophia tells me the school has a court. It will be great to play against someone who can keep up with me.

I can't wait to see you. I think you and I are going to have SO much fun!

Reiko!!!☺

31901055789640